Noah Changes Me

By S L Wall

<u>Chapter 1</u>

In the rolling hills of Northern Wales there was a small town called East Tridam. It was a beautiful quiet small town with about 1,000 people in total East Tridam is situated in an area with three dams on the east side hence the town name, on the West side there is a hillside with a big forest that many of the town folk use while taking nice walks in the summertime. There is also a large grassy area which is situated at the back of the forest where people from the town and the surrounding areas and villages and even total strangers just visiting the area come to camp there while taking a holiday use the large wide open spaces to have a break in the refreshing open air, enjoy having a family picnic and maybe stay and camp there for a few days so that they can enjoy the peace and tranquillity as well as taking a long well-earned rest. The North side is a mountain which is quite steep and only good for the mountaineers and experienced climbers from amongst the town folk and visitors. The South side of the town as a little road with just enough room for two-way traffic in which both sides of the roads are lined with tall trees and small rocky mountain sides. At Christmas time t when there are festivals and special holidays the congregation of the local St John's Church and towns folk decorated the trees with lights. To make the town look more cheerful and inviting.

East Tridam at one time was one of the best places to stay for visiting youth groups as it had loads of exciting things for them, mountaineering, rambling, and the occasional treasure hunt. The town, although it was small, it was just like any normal town with its own school, cinema, accountant, solicitors, grocers and a post office as well as a wide selection of other shops and best of all was *Nora's Kitchen* run by Noah's wife, everyone came from miles around to eat some of her special apple pie and cakes,

Noah and his sons Simon, Harry and Joseph who were triplets, when weather permitted would take the youth group to the big lake which was situated on the other side of the picnic area to fish and use the time to tell them about the fishermen from the bible when Jesus called them to be his disciples. Jesus asked them to stop fishing for fish follow him and taught them to be fishers of men, as with everything and everybody else Noah and Nora got older and Noah needed to stop taking the groups out, but any groups that did come to fish and hear stories, Noah relied on his sons to carry on and take them out when they were not working at the family haulage business. If the occasion arrived there would always be cover for them anyway.

Nora was getting on too, but she kept on cooking with the help of her daughter-in-law's Sharon, Hannah and Joan when they were not working at the haulage yard and other jobs for the town folk and whatever visitors came although that number slowly decreased as soon as the Casino was open.

Now everything has changed in East Tridam as the *Arrow Hat Casino* brought in a different kind of people and a far more bad element and visitors. The genuine law-abiding citizens of the town stayed away from that part of East Tridam since Jonah Whey came back to town after his time in prison with loads of money in his pocket and a swagger in his walk as if he was some kind of royalty and began to open up his Casino.

Jonah Whey is a 5ft 11inches tall man and he weighs about 15 stones, clean shaven and always walked around the town in a white silk suit black shirt and a white tie with an arrow and hat printed on it and perfectly shined black shoes. Jonah is always walking around East Tridam as if he owned the town with a swagger in his step and to help him run things like (drugs, prostitution, gambling and blackmail). He has a small band of workers who he calls the hunters, started life as haulage drivers for Noah until they were attracted by the idea of earning copious amounts of money for fighting as well as killing and getting away with it. The hunters doubled as workers in the Casino as his dealers and bouncers. If anyone crosses the line the hunters would hunt you down and shoot you dead as if you were animals. Jonah's upbringing was not bad at all in fact when he was a small lad everyone in the town thought he was a little angel. The old ladies used to walk up to him, squeeze his cheeks which at first was ok but soon he really started to hate it so much.

Jonah's parents were never there for him and he walked around in torn and worn clothes that never looked as if they were being washed at all and shoes with soles that could talk to you? Jonah's parents did not show any love for Jonah growing up. All they cared about was their next drink and when they drank they would argue. All he needed to do was go home after school and ask for something to eat and for asking he would get a good beating so at first when he asked for a snack he hid thinking he was going to be hit which shocked Nora greatly. On the other hand, if anyone ever needed a hand or assistance Jonah would always be there first. Things changed in a big way for Jonah as he grew up. Noah and Nora had three sons Simon Harry and Joseph who were also the same age as Jonah, and in the same class as them as well, so as Noah had always brought up his sons to treat everyone as they would like to be treated themselves, so they helped Jonah and brought him home for meals after school. When Nora saw what, he was wearing she was so upset she gave him some of their son's clothes and started to give him the care and attention every boy needed while growing up.

The first-time Jonah went home in brand new clean clothes and new shoes both of Jonah's parents went straight round in a totally drunk state rowing with Noah and Nora shouting it's their place to decide what Jonah wore and not them." If you both expect us to pay you for these clothes you have another think coming. Just because you are la de dah in the church and have a business you both think you run this town, but you don't". In fact, in the eyes of strangers it looked like Nora had 4 sons.

Every Sunday Jonah joined their family and went to church with them Jonah joined Simon, Harry and Joseph in the church choir. When all four of the lads had finished school, Noah changed the name of his business to *No Work 2 Hard proprietors Noah & Sons* and Said to Jonah I have spoken to my boys and they all agree where it says sons that means it will also include you too. As well as this surprise for Jonah he was also given a supervisory position and given a small team of his own to lead which eventually became the start of his gang of the hunters.

Everything started to change at work from then on as Jonah started feeling a little put out. To him it seemed that he was the only one working all hours of the day and only getting a minimum wage when Noah was not even turning up as he helped at their local church and his Sons kept disappearing to take groups out. So, when a stranger who he met while doing yet another long overnight lorry drive gave him a way to make lots of money with hardly any work, he automatically jumped at the chance. The Stranger who introduced himself as Zach Taxma gave Jonah an address and asked him to deliver a small box to this address little did Jonah know but this was the start of a whole different kind of adventure.

Jonah delivered the small box quite easily and when he saw how much money he was paid his eyes sparkled. All Jonah could see was pound note signs in front of his eyes and he was loving it, as he would need work all week to get that much cash and it only took him 1 hour from then on Jonah was hooked. Later that week Jonah had a phone call which asked him if he wanted to make another delivery but a little bigger this time and without even thinking Jonah said *A BIG YES*. Zach gave Jonah time to think about it before asking him again explaining the bigger the delivery the bigger the payday, but it comes with a higher risk. Jonah did not care he just liked the idea of money, money and more money.

The problem was when he took delivery of the box it was getting late, so he left it in the back of the truck and texted Zach on his mobile saying he would deliver it first thing the next day. Zach texted back and finally agreed, that when it all started to go seriously wrong, the town would never be the same again. From then on, that night Noah and the boys stayed late to check all the trucks to see if any of them needed repairs ready to be updated or renewed if required. Inside Jonah's truck to their surprise they noticed the box and not knowing the contents as it was not listed on any delivery sheet, on opening it they were all shocked to see the packets of unknown white power inside.

That night as Noah and his family who were all law-abiding citizens were concerned Noah and his Sons after praying long and hard decided he would contact the police that were outside of their town as they did not fully trust their police. Also, the delivery address was not in their town, so they contacted that police station with his sons hearing the call, resealed the box so it looked the exact same way as they found it, they arranged to have Jonah followed the next day so when the box was delivered everyone present was arrested. Jonah was not happy at being arrested so at first, he turned around mocking the police which did not help, saying you are too fat and ugly, catch me but after Jonah had been running for a couple of minutes and saw the police were right behind him decided running was not the answer. So, using none of his high IQ decided to turn around and take the policemen head on but Jonah ended up in more trouble as the policeman was stronger and smarter and made it look so easy to overcome Jonah without them both even breaking sweat. Within minutes Jonah was being held down and handcuffs applied. After a couple of minutes another policeman joined them with the police car and with the help of the two police Jonah who was getting mad and struggled quite a bit was helped to his feet, while one officer opened the door the other one lowered Jonah in the back of the car.

In the car ride, back to the police station Jonah's mood did not change. in fact, the nearer they got the cockier he got saying "you two will be picking up your P45 as when I get there I will have the pair of you sued for beating me up. Also, these charges will not stick as I'm innocent and you have no proof". When they arrived at the station the officer helped Jonah out of the car making sure the car door swung back on him, after the door hit him some more police cars arrived with their prisoners from the raid. One female officer shouted over" Darling did I not tell you someone would have an accident with that hole there". Jonah Stared at both the officers. After that Jonah was ushered into a waiting area as the custody area was very busy. Everyone from that drugs raid was glaring at each other trying to work out who tipped the police off but not one of them looked scared. One by one the prisoners were let inside Zach and Jonah were the last two until Zach was let in first, so all the suspicion was on Jonah's shoulders. Jonah was very scared about the whole event, so he tried to act the big man by refusing to stand up when he was called but right next to him was a very kind officer who personally helped Jonah to his feet, also another officer stood nearby just in case he needed assistance in walking to where the Custody Sergeant was waiting but Jonah looked straight at him, nodded and walked by himself. The Custody Sergeant a Sergeant Gideon Safe asked Jonah politely his name, age and date of birth but as Jonah was trying to be tough, looked straight at the Sergeant seeing his name tag Gideon Safe he started to Laugh out loud which annoyed the PC as he was Nathaniel Safe the sergeant's brother, The Custody Sergeant raised his hand and said Nath its ok, asking again he said in a stronger tone name address date of birth. At this point Jonah realised he lost standing tall he said, "name Jonah

Whey". Before any more details were given Gideon Safe looked at his brother and they both laughed, Jonah tried get free from his handcuffs but could not shouting "what's wrong with you"? "why are you laughing at my name?", the Pc Safe said "what's wrong. You not like been laughed at because of your name". Sergeant Safe said "that's enough. Stating your name is Jonah Whey it's just it sounds like going away and mate you are going away for sure".

When the fun had stopped, and the questions were finished Jonah was ushered into a small room to have a DNA swab done then a group of photos first from the front then right profile followed lastly by the left profile finally they took a full set of fingers prints after all that was done Jonah had his first taste of what was to come as he was locked up in a police cell waiting to be questioned. As Jonah was walking to his cell the cockiness started back shouting as he walked "The grass is dead when I get you", Jonah refused a solicitor as he insisted that he was innocent as only guilty people have solicitors. After waiting nearly all night finally a DCI Arthur Pain introduced himself and seeing Jonah starting to grin (Jonah still trying to be cocky) said "Yes the other Arthur pain is that copper who arrested me." After that DCI Pain lifted one finger and without saying another word Jonah was quiet. In the interview room Jonah was given his rights and cautioned again as the DC asked him questions. Jonah kept looking round the room saying "No comment can I go now" after about 1 hour of hearing this Jonah was sent back to his cell. Three hours later the custody sergeant asked Jonah to stand behind the yellow line and began to formally charge him with possession with attempt to supply. "As you have nowhere to live as your previous abode do not want you living there we have no option but to hold you in custody till your court date", It was not just Jonah. Everyone who was there including Zach was sent to prison to await trial for drug possession and smuggling.

When the court day arrived, Noah was there to keep an eye on Jonah and to try and find out why he did such a thing. He asked him, if possible, what drove him to breaking the law when he made him a part of his family. Jonah was sentenced to 5 years in Larkswood Prison in London. When he entered the prison and shown to his cell to Jonah is amazement he was to share with a real hard career criminal who was in there serving a multiple life sentence for murder. He was a hitman for a major drug cartel; the prisoner was called Derek Edward Ville. He was a tall man about 6ft tall and 18 stones, shaved head and clean shaven with a scar over his right eye. When he removed his shirt, he was covered from head to toe in tattoos. While the prison staff there were trying to teach Jonah the right way to behave to aid in his rehabilitation, in which Jonah sat there listening and smiling, nodding every now and then as if he was
really interested and sorry for what he did as well as in what they were saying,

just because he was told if he agreed to go to all these classes it would help him get initial release.

The main problem with what the prison staff were trying to get Jonah to listen to went in one ear and out the other. As the cell door shut for the night Derek would teach Jonah a different kind of lesson in which Jonah preferred the kind of lessons Derek was teaching. As Jonah now had a taste of being rich he liked it and was willing to do anything to be rich again.

Derek at first did not say too much to Jonah as he was not sure if he was a plant or not but after a few months started to talk to Jonah to find out what he was in there for. Jonah was a little naive but noticing how Derek was treated by the other prisoners and how some of the prison officers treated Derek like royalty, he found this amusing. As Jonah was his cell mate he was treated the same way. Jonah opened up a little and explained how he got caught. At first Derek laughed but a few days later asked him if he knew what he did wrong, this puzzled Jonah a little so for the next couple of nights no one spoke. The prison wardens one day got on Jonah's nerves and made him mad so as soon as Jonah got to his cell for the night and the doors shut he shouted at Derek saying, "if you are so smart you tell me what I did wrong".

While waiting for Jonah to calm down a little Derek said "sit down as from now on your proper rehabilitation will begin if you really want it and by the way, don't ever speak to me again like that. One more murder means nothing to me if you get me", after saying this Derek gave a wicked grin. Jonah looked at Derek and apologised quickly. On hearing. proper rehabilitation this interested Jonah so much his ears pricked up. After being told he did something the wrong way half of Jonah's mind was on what could he have done different whilst the other part was what does he know? If Derek knew so much why he was in here for multiple murders and not free as a bird but Jonah re thought about it as he was interested in staying alive. After Jonah had refocused Derek asked Jonah to go through everything again bit by bit and he would explain what he should have done if he was clever as he thinks he is.

Jonah sat down and began by saying how Zach approached him asking if he wanted to make some easy cash, Derek replied "did you know Zach? was he undercover? You should have checked him out first. "Jonah carried on" After that first delivery my eyes sparkled at the cash I got so without thinking when the offer for more came I jumped in straight away. Derek asked did you think of asking to see his boss first before doing more deliveries? Secondly never leave stuff like drugs in your work vehicle. You should have moved it to a different place then the next day picked it up before you delivered it. Jonah was getting a little mad now as Derek was talking to him like he was a child. Derek continued in the morning "did you think about checking the lock on your lorry. I bet you didn't". Jonah was getting very mad at this and said "Can we carry this on tomorrow? I need to think" Derek nodded. That night Jonah did not sleep after hearing Derek and started to think what a fool he was getting caught. It was three days later when Jonah and Derek carried on as the next day one of the prisoners an Andrew Nutt thought he was big enough to kill Derek Edward Ville on his own but Jonah who wanted to act big like Derek and also be known as a big hard man. As Andrew walked up to Derek Jonah noticed a shiny object in Andrew's hand, thinking it was a knife he walked up to him, punched Andrew once knocking him out, so Jonah then ended up in solitary as punishment,

When Jonah had finished his three days in solitary and went back to his cell Derek wanted to know why he punched Andrew Nutt. After Jonah explained the reason Derek went quiet. After a few minutes Derek gave out a mad and crazy laugh. Later that day Derek knew he could now trust Jonah more and from that moment it was time for Jonah's real education, Derek carried on and walked through a few steps that would mean next time Jonah would be more brainier and be smarter. The steps Derek gave him were.

- Always ask to see the boss before doing a deal
- If not able to see boss be the boss
- Meet people in a place where escape is easy
- Always get some other person to take the risk
- Buy the services of the right people
- Never get caught

Jonah liked this advice. When it was time for him to leave Derek slipped a note to him with a few contacts that were going be of use for Jonah to start afresh. The only difference would be if Jonah took Derek's advice and assistance and journeyed on this road there would be no way back for him. Jonah did not care he just saw pound note signs and nothing else;

After 3 years inside Jonah was released for good behaviour. He did not return straight away to East Tridam. Instead he stayed in and around London to gather himself some collateral for him to start his new career.

Five years later Jonah had enough of London as it was getting a little hot and dangerous for him to stay much longer anyway so he then decided to travel back to East Tridam. On his way there he met a gentleman that knew Jonah from a contact he knew in London. The gentleman wanted to buy some cocaine from him, so Jonah sold him £100 worth and he added that to his money all ready to make his grand entrance back in to East Tridam a more elaborate one. When Jonah arrived in town the first thing he needed to do was go to the police station to report his address. After a few weeks of living in a bed and breakfast Jonah brought an old warehouse. While still in the bed and breakfast he started building his casino.

The best thing was when he entered the police station to report in where he was staying so the probation officer in London knew his whereabouts he had the biggest surprise he could have as the Police Inspector was none other than the gentleman that brought the cocaine from him, so Jonah thought all his Christmases had come at once. Now anything Jonah wanted to do he knew he could get away with as he had only just got back to town and he already owned the police, so his criminal empire had now begun. The gentleman who brought the cocaine was none other than.

The Inspector Saul Hardman. He was a well-built man in his early 50's but looked older he was 6ft 4inches tall black hair with a black goatee. It was black, but you could tell he dyed it as it didn't look natural. Saul was married to a lovely woman called Sarah who was in her 40's with long blonde hair about 6ft tall and had the figure every man in the town would die to be with. They had two daughters, Martha 19 years old and Mary 16 years old. They both had long blonde hair and looked just like their mother. The only thing was that Sarah got Saul into trying cocaine at a party they attended in London and now they both cannot stop taking it and they are both now totally hooked but the one good thing is they *NEVER* take it in front of their daughters.

To keep up with paying for their drugs Saul kept on visiting Jonah for a cut of his illegal activities by turning his back when it was going ahead. To keep him quiet Saul however gave any money he earned back to Jonah as he always gambled it away on blackjack or poker in the casino to make more money for his and his wife's cocaine habit, but he was a terrible gambler and always lost it all before he left which Jonah also used this to his advantage and this kept him always in debt to Jonah.

When Jonah took this way of earning as a living never went to the side of the town where Noah and his family lived and worked unless he wanted to recruit more of Noah's drivers to further his criminal empire. On one occasion Noah saw Jonah come to his business and asked him directly "why did you turn out the way you did as he and his wife brought you up differently", Jonah thanked Noah in a rude and sarcastic way and when he got more people to join his gang of hunters he turned around laughed and left ignoring Noah and his lads. He refused to enter that part of the town in case Noah tried again to convert him back to the sweet little angel he once was. Although Jonah was this big man now and ran every illegal thing in East Tridam Noah and his family scared him greatly.

Chapter 2

Noah was an old man in his mid-60's. He was of a small build with grey hair and his balance was not 100% and now needed the use of a walking stick to get around, so after spending a long time thinking he decided it was now time for him to semi retire and turn over most of the running of the family haulage business to his three sons. They were in fact triplets but each looked slightly different in features. Simon was 5ft 6inches and very muscly and had a thick head of brown hair, Harry was very muscly too and 5ft 10inches tall but he had a bald head and a thick black beard, however, Joseph was the odd one out as he was a very tall 6ft 5inches tall with blonde hair and wore glasses.

Simon and Harry were the brawny ones in the family whereas Joseph was more of the brains and for some strange reason it worked well, so Noah knew the family haulage business would be in safe hands and would be a growing and successful business in the future for a very long time to come.

Noah could now spend more of his time doing things he enjoyed in his local church and serving God when he was able to that is, Noah started to attend the local church since he was a very small lad, about the same age as he and his wife Nora took their small boys and at the end of the year he would be celebrating being a member for 60yrs. At St Johns Church he saw many a new vicar come and go. At the moment the new vicar was a young man who preferred to be known as a pastor and not as a vicar, his name was Pastor Adam Christus in which the Latin translation of Christus is Christ. Adam Christus was a tall man, 6ft 6inches and very thin his hair was short blonde cropped close to his head and he was always perfectly clean shaven. His wife was called Evelyn but preferred to be called Eve and she was not the normal type of vicar's wife, she had short hair that was coloured pink and she also had a piercing in the bottom of her lip. She also had a thin figure and was 5ft 2ins tall but when she joined her husband by playing the organ Wow!!! the way she played was amazing. It was as if the keys sang the song to you.

The church was a traditional one with a bell tower that rang 1hr before the service started to let everyone in East Tridam know that they had 1hr to get themselves into the right frame and to help prepare themselves to worship God. Inside the church it was totally different as it looked more of a modern building since Pastor Adam Christus had joined the parish the song that were sung were also more modern as he played them on his guitar with his wife joining him by playing the organ as well as singing.

The pastor was very happy to have Noah's assistance to help with the day to day running of the church especially when the church was at its busiest which was between September and December.

As the schools went back it was harvest time then end of October it was

Halloween in which the church ran light parties for the children to combat the evil associated with Halloween. After that had finished it was time to begin the preparations ready for the school children coming to the church for their Christmas services. As well as that Adam and Noah had the church's own Christmas services to prepare and get ready for.

During this time of year Nora, Noah's wife hardly saw her husband, Nora was also in her late 60's. She was a very dainty looking lady but always had her longish grey hair neatly tied back and her hair was always like that. When she was not feeling 100% her hair was always tied back with a scrunch that matched her dress.

Sunday was the only time that the family were able to spend time together but even then, some Sundays were busier than others especially as occasionally Noah spoke at the Sunday morning service.

This particular Sunday when it was time for Noah to speak he got up from his usual seat walked gingerly up to the lectern and began to read the passage from his New International Version Bible. Noah spoke on **Philippians 4 verse 10-20.**

"10 I rejoiced in the Lord that at last you renewed your concern for me. Indeed, you were concerned but you had no opportunity to show it. 11 I am not saying this because I am not in need. For I have learned to be content whatever the circumstance. 12 I know what is it to be in need, and I know what it is to have plenty. I have learned the secret of being in content in any situation, whatever well fed or hungry, whatever living in plenty or in want. 13 I can do all things through him who gives me strength. 14 Yet it was good of you to share in my troubles. 15 Moreover, as you Philippians know, in the early days of your acquaintance with the gospel. When I set out from Macedonia, not one church shared with me in the matter of giving and receiving, except you only. 16 for even when I was in Thessalonica you sent me aid more than once when I was in need. 17 not that I

desire your gifts: what I desire is more be credited to your account. 18 I have received full payment and have more than enough. I am amply supplied, now that I have received from Epadphroditus the gifts you sent. They are a fragrant offering an acceptable sacrifice, pleasing to God. 19 And my God will meet all your needs according to the riches of his glory in Christ Jesus 20 to our God and father be glory for ever and ever Amen".

Noah stood silent for a few minutes then before he spoke on the passage he had just read prayed out loud

Thank you, God, for giving us this passage and please give me your servant the words to speak but do not make them my words but use me as a vessel for me to speak your words in your holy name Amen.

After everyone could say Amen themselves if they wanted to Noah waited a few seconds to let the words of his prayer sink in before he started to preach.

"In the passage. I just read Paul was happy that the people cared and worried about him but they were unsure how or when they were going to show their worries and concerns about his wellbeing. Paul did not worry about any of this as he knew God had already taken care of everything even before he asked for it.

God can take care of anyone who asks in his name but will only give us what he thinks is necessary not what we want e.g: he will not provide us with a three-course meal if our stomach can only take a sandwich.

Paul learnt very early on Gods power and glory and his holy presence will be there if only we ask.

Paul also knew that in whatever place he travelled to God was in front, behind and at his side. If the love of God was not there he would let Paul know in some way, for me and you the main lesson for us all comes from verse 13 of the book of Philippians I read earlier and that is "I can do all things through him who gives me strength" and that's the main thing that we all can remember in our daily lives. Everything is possible if we let God guide us for with God in our lives we will be rich in his glory for ever and ever Amen"

After the church service had finished and they had a cup of tea while chatting to everyone. Noah, Nora and their sons Simon, Harry and Joseph along with their wives Sharon, Hannah and Joan in which it was quite strange and a little funny as their wives were also triplets. Sharon who was married to Joseph was 5ft 2inches and had long black hair. Her figure was very straight and she wore contact lenses as she did not want to wear glasses as she felt uncomfortable. She worked in the office alongside her husband. The main thing that got these two together was that they were brilliant on computers and sometimes Noah thought they actually made the office computers talk, they were that good, Hannah was married to Simon. She had short black hair and was 5ft 9inches tall and was the only women employed as a Haulage Driver and the main thing about Hannah was she could out lift any man especially her husband. Joan was married to Harry. She also had short black hair but was only 5ft tall and the only unique thing about Joan was she was the only one that did not work full time for the haulage yard but she did handle their accounts.

When they had finished chatting they all went back to Noah and Nora's bungalow. They moved there when their three boys left home for their own comfort. The bungalow was very nice and small, just big enough for the two of them but not to small that they could not entertain. The bungalow had a white painted front with a small lawn so they could sit outside in the summer. Inside they had quite a large kitchen with room for a big dining table. The kitchen itself was fully fitted with an arga stove and fitted kitchen cupboards with a wooden finish. A couple of the fitted cupboards which were designed to hold plates had a glass portion in which it had a leaded design to make them look different. The living room was smaller with oak beams showing on the ceiling and in the centre of the main wall was a small wood burning fire. On cold winter nights with the door shut it was brilliant and warm. As soon as they all got inside Nora and the ladies went in to the kitchen to assist Nora in cooking the lunch while the men went into the living room to talk business.

When Nora had got everything that was needed out of the cupboard for the lunch she checked on the joint of beef that had been cooking slowly in the oven while they were all in church. Without Nora even saying a word Sharon, Hannah and Joan asked what she wanted the rest of them to do in preparing the food. Everything else was already split between the ladies as if they knew without been told. Hannah was on vegetable duty which meant peeling and cutting carrots, Sharon was on potato duty which was quite a big job as they always had both roast and mashed potato and that just left Joan who with Nora's supervision and guidance was on dessert duty as no one knew how to make a perfect apple and rhubarb crumble better than Nora. Joan's came close which was why she was on dessert duty but something Nora did just maked it taste that much better. After everyone had finished their jobs and everything was cooking away Nora drained the goodness from the bottom of the joint of roast beef putting the joint on a plate to rest. With the goodness from the joint of roasted beef Nora made the juices the base of the best and ultimate gravy, when she finished making the gravy it had little tiny flecks of the meat goodness flowing through it which makes the gravy so much more tasty and enjoyable.

While this was going on in the kitchen Simon, Harry and Joseph were in the living room talking with their dad. Noah was sitting very comfortable in his special white leather recliner chair that only he was allowed to sit on but as per usual so far through their business chats Noah got so comfortable that he dozed off. Knowing this Joseph made notes of all their conversations so their Dad could read them later and let them know what he thought.

Unknowing to the lads and the ladies in the kitchen Noah was dreaming and that dream would not only change their lives but every single person in East Tridam as well.

"Noah was deep in the land of dream and as he woke or what he thought was him awake he found himself standing outside a big building that was full of offices in his Sunday best grey suit white shirt and a red tie. Noah knew it was a big office building as when he entered he could see the board with a list of about 30 different companies on it.

Noah put his hand in his left side pocket and pulled out a piece of paper with a name of the company that when he looked on the board it was down on the list on the first floor. The company was Highest

*Power Consultants chief executive as
being Mr Graham Odd so Noah
walked towards the lift and went to
the first floor when he got there to his
surprise there was only one office
there and the rest was open plan but
no one was at the desks. On
approaching the office before he
could knock on the door it
mysteriously opened so Noah walked
in and saw two gentlemen sitting at
one end of the table. As soon as he
entered Noah was welcomed in and
offered a seat it was then one of the
gentlemen introduced himself as
Graham Odd and then he introduced
the other gentleman as his personal
assistant as Mr James Zeus.*

*Graham was about 70 years old
with a full head of perfectly combed
grey hair and a grey beard. He was
about 5ft 6inches tall and the
strange thing Noah saw was his
personal assistant looked the same,
only younger but had black hair.
Noah sat down and James offered*

him a drink to which he said "water would be fine". After all the pleasantries were over Noah asked why he was here and not at home enjoying his lunch. Graham said he would tell you everything when you are ready.

Noah replied quickly OK I am ready. Noah I have been watching and note that you and your family truly love God and as for that you have been chosen to be saved. God would like to build an ark or as you would say a big boat to keep you and your family safe as there is going be a flood, you will also take with you two of every land animal. Noah looked strangely and said you are kidding me. Is this a candid camera show I'm on? Graham and James said together NO. After a while Graham tried to continue but Noah jumped in and said how am I supposed to build a boat? I am too old to even put a new gate on without help and the instructions

*and anyway I'm a retired haulage
driver I do not know anything about
boats.*

*James then said its ok Noah calm
down. All you will need will be
posted to you tomorrow on a tablet
like this. Noah then said sure and
how big will this boat be then.
Graham said not that big. The
dimensions are 450ft long x 75ft high
x 45ft wide or if you prefer 135
metres long x 22.5 metres high x
13.5 metres wide. Noah's reply was
in a loud voice and he said "WHAT?"*
at that moment Noah woke up quickly
and saw that everyone had rushed in to
see what was up.

Noah apologised and promised to
explain his actions after they had eaten
their lunch as the smell coming from the
kitchen smelt so divine and it was
making him even hungrier than he was
before. After they all were seated
around their large round mahogany solid
wood table with matching chairs that the
children brought Noah and Nora when

they moved to their bungalow Noah said a thankful prayer.

Dear Lord
Thank you for giving us the strength to carry out your work and giving us the skills we use especially we thank you for the food you have provided for us to enjoy in your holy name
AMEN

When everyone has said Amen Noah sliced the roast beef and Nora passed the plates around serving herself and Noah last the rest of the food were all in dishes in the middle of the tables that the ladies kindly brought through from the kitchen so that everyone could help themselves. It also helped with communication and giving the meal a more family sharing atmosphere. Nora and Noah loved the fact it was a round table as it gave the impression that everyone is equal just as in their Christian life they believe whatever colour or creed everyone should be treated the same. One thing was a certainty and that was every time they meet as a family for a meal the dishes always came to the table full and left the dining table empty.

When everyone had finished eating the lunch Nora with the help from Hannah and Joan went into the kitchen to bring out the apple and rhubarb crumble and custard. When they all had polished off their crumble and custard in which although he said he was full Joseph had seconds. Simon got his dads attention and reminded him that he promised an explanation of his strange outburst from earlier before lunch.

Noah then said. "So I did thank you Simon for reminding me while I was sitting down as usual I fell asleep and had a very strange dream that was so realistic that it was kind of scary". Noah looked around and asked them to promise that he could finish telling them the whole dream before they reacted in which with a worrying look on all their faces they agreed.

Noah ushered everyone to the living room asking them to sit down after everyone had sat down Noah paced around the floor a little and after a while stood tall and straight as if he was about to preach a sermon and told them his dream trying not miss out any details.

I dozed off and when what I thought was awake I was actually asleep I found myself outside a large building. On entering I stood in front of a glass entrance door and saw I was wearing my Sunday best grey suit and a red tie. When I looked around I noticed a large board with a list of offices and business. I put my hand in the left pocket of my suit and found a piece of paper and on it was a name of a company, the company name was Highest Power Consultants Chief Executive Mr Graham Odd, so I then looked on the list and found out it was on the first floor. I entered and on finding a lift went inside pressed the 1st floor and waited. When the lift arrived to my shock it was an open plan office with a load of empty desks and at the far end just one office, I walked slowly up to the office and as I was about to

*knock on the door it magically
opened. On going inside I found two
people sitting at a large desk, the
older of the two gentlemen stood up
and said "Welcome we have been
expecting you Noah". I stood
amazed. The gentleman then
apologised and said my name is
Graham Odd and the gentleman
sitting there is my Personal Assistant
Mr James Zeus. At that point James
jumped up and shook my hand and
asked if I wanted a drink. I have not
even begun telling you the weird part
yet at which point* Harry jumped in and
said, "there is weirder to come", *Noah
said I asked you before I started to
what?* Harry apologized and said "carry
on Dad", *Noah cleared his throat and
carried on, Graham then said "let me
tell you why you are here, in East
Tridam it has become a very evil
place to live so God has decided a
flood will cover it all but do not worry
has he wants you to build a ark or
what they call now a boat to keep*

you and your family safe and you are to take with you 2 of every land animal", I stood there laughing and told them I know nothing about building a boat in which James jumped in and said I was not to worry as a tablet will be delivered tomorrow with all the details I need to know and that's when you heard me shout "NO!"

Everyone looked as if someone had just slapped them hard and then they all laughed as if Noah was trying out a comedy routine on them. Noah then said in a loud voice, I THOUGHT AS YOU AT FIRST do but listen Simon get that piece of paper and write down the two names I mentioned, Mr Graham Odd and Mr James Zeus but write the second name underneath on the same line as Mr Graham Odd write Mr GODD on the same line as Mr James Zeus write Mr J ZEUS and then pass it around so everyone can see. After everyone had seen it Noah then said" what does everyone see". No one spoke then Joseph said with a startle, "I see something but it looks weird", Nora said "just say it as we have heard far more weirder things already so one more is no problem".

Joseph stood up next to his dad and said "Does no one else see it in dad's dream? The two people in the office were in fact GOD AND JESUS as well as that HIGHEST POWER CONSULTANTS the dream is God speaking to us just so we do in fact know it's right if the tablet comes tomorrow I think we should do as we have been asked and wait till tomorrow". Simon and Harry both agreed. At that point Nora suggested they all went home so they could discuss it in private and they should come for lunch the next day to discuss further.

When everyone left Nora told Noah whatever he decides she will back him 100%. I think for now let's pray and read the bible for wisdom and confirmation. So they sat down and Nora said she knew the perfect passage and that was Genesis 6 v1 to Genesis 8 v19, the story of Noah's Ark to see how he managed to cope and maybe it could help them prepare and Noah agreed. That night Noah could not sleep that much. Early that morning they were both woken by the parcel van arriving with a parcel addressed to Noah from Highest Power Consultants.

Chapter 3

That Sunday afternoon as Simon, Harry
and Joseph were walking home with
their wives they let their wives walk a
little in front so they could have a quiet
conversation between themselves. At
first their conversation was about their
dad and was he ok or going crazy now
that he is getting old. After they passed
over that conversation knowing full well
that there was a more better chance of
them going crazy first than their dad.
The conversation moved on to the
dream that their dad had spoken about.

Simon started by asking Joseph if he
knew what would a big boat or as their
dad pronounced it as an ark would
actually cost to build. Joseph was quiet
for a few minutes and said he would
look into it and text them later when he
had done some working out and worked
on a rough estimate so they could use it
as a guide line.

While the men were talking about how
to help their dad the women's
conversation was quite different as they

were discussing more about what effect it would have on them and the things that they would need to do without if their husbands were to help with their father's crazy and mental idea. The one thing that all of the three ladies Hannah, Sharon and Joan agreed to was totally un-Christian and that was they were being self-centred and only thinking about I and not us as being part of a family that were all Christians. They should know there is no I IN TEAM and being part of a family they should all work as 1 team. In their case they were being 100% selfish and not thinking in a pure and God like nature.

When they arrived at their own homes it was deadly silent at first then Simon started off the conversation with his wife Hannah by at first stating that the house that they are living in was bought by his dad as a wedding gift and if he wanted to mortgage it to help his dad he could do, Hannah stared that hard it was as if Simon had been pushed. Simon fell back and sat down as Hannah started to talk.

Hannah started by reminding Simon of all the things he promised. As Simon sat down Hannah towered over him and started to work down an imaginary list, at that point Simon did not dare speak a word:

- We were going have a holiday to remember
- You said you would redecorate the whole house
- Buy new furniture to match the new décor
- Update our car

Hannah then said in a tearful manner "Now all that you promised me you were going do is not going to happen so you can help your crazy old father with an even crazier so called dream he had and that you don't love me anymore". Simon let Hannah finish before he jumped up and on raising his voice saying "Hannah if the shoe was on the other foot and we needed help with as you said a crazy dream who would be first to help us." Hannah said in a low and this time she was really near to crying which was a very hard thing to do is make Hannah cry but she looked ready to cry and in a sweet and solemn voice almost as if it was a whisper "your Dad". Simon then stormed out of the room and went in to his study banging the door behind him. After a couple of hours you could not hear a pin drop as Hannah knocked on the study door, walked inside, asked Simon if he wanted something to eat or drink and quietly kissed her husband on the cheek and said "Sorry" and agreed that they would help anyway they could with his father's plan. Just as she said that Simon's iPhone 6 pinged and a message from Joseph appeared.

When Harry and Joan arrived home before Harry had even got in to their house to remove his jacket Joan hit him full pelt with both barrels saying in a definite and stern tone in her voice "listen here you, I am going give you two options and you had better make the right choice"

- Help your crazy dad and me and you are over

- Think of us and our future we can sell up move away and you can start your own haulage company.

Harry was so mad his face was turning red. All he did was point his finger at Joan and then to a chair then in a very loud voice said, "SIT DOWN AND SHUT IT I AM SPEAKING NOW." After Harry calmed down a little bit he started to speak. saying almost the same as Simon stating, "When we first got married I asked my dad for a deposit for this house and he ended up saying "no I will buy you a house call it a wedding gift" and if he decided to help his dad with whatever weird or crazy plan he as then if God has asked him to build a boat then we will be right next to him helping, ok? At that point Joan stood up and said I will get you the spare bedding as you are sleeping in the spare room until you change your mind or at least start seeing things straight. That made Harry very angry shouting back at Joan saying, "Remember who brought us this house, so I hope you enjoy the spare room until you see straight" At that second a text came through on his mobile phone from Joseph.

When Joseph and Sharon arrived home their conversation went a little different as the second they got in Joseph said I'm going work on how much this dream of my dad's will cost him and his family too.

Sharon raised her point by just saying "Ok but don't you forget what you promised me about redecorating the house". Joseph said "I know but that can wait because if this dream of my dad's is true we could end up not having a house to live in never mind to re decorate. As Christians should we not be thinking at this time of WWJD (what would Jesus do)? We should as Christians think what Jesus would expect us to do when challenges are given to us in his name."

Joseph started right away working away on his HP ProBook 6560b laptop to try and work out every possible costing, trying to make the cheapest possible cost by splitting the cost between himself Simon and Harry for the cost of materials and manpower required to build the ark/boat. After a couple of hours Sharon went into the study where Joseph was working to bring him something to eat and a drink, Sharon

Spoke in a kindly voice saying "Joseph, it's getting on. Why not take a break, eat something and then text your brother saying you will bring the information tomorrow at lunch so you can all discuss it properly" After Sharon had finished talking she kissed Joseph on the side of his cheek and said "I can see that you want to help your dad well you can count me in as well 100%. Now you need eat and take a break because we all will need ours and Gods strength to do this". Joseph ate, finished off the costing and texted Simon, Harry and his dad saying that he would bring all the paperwork to the lunch meeting.

The next day early that morning Joseph got up and went straight to his study to check over the working out he did the night before. Simon and Harry were up early as well as they had early deliveries to make but promised that they would definitely be back in time for lunch. At Lunch Nora prepared enough food that most people would have at a party as she knew everyone would be hungry and she also had a funny feeling that the family meeting could take quite a long time. As everyone was up early and Noah and Nora were up because of when the parcel arrived Nora used the time to make the lunch a buffet type lunch so they could eat while they talked. The only thing was Nora prepared everything any normal person would think it was a party and not a family meeting/lunch. There were plates of sandwiches, cakes, biscuits, sausages on sticks and cheese & pineapple, mini pizzas and quiches. Also, as they discussed things through it would be in some relaxed as possible surroundings.

When they all arrived they were totally shocked as the food was all laid out on the dining table. There was that much food there was no room for anything else, the seating was also sorted in a circle with a solid mahogany coffee table in the centre with a parcel placed in the middle unopened from HIGHEST POWER CONSULTANTS.

When everyone had taken their seat they all stared at the parcel that was placed on the coffee table until Noah said a prayer of thankfulness for the lovely spread of food and also for guidance for whatever was waiting for them in the box had planned for them. After Noah had finished saying the prayer he waited a few minutes to keep them all in suspense a little longer then he picked up the parcel and opened it carefully took the tablet out of the box and after picking the tablet up looked all around the outside looking a little confused and said out loud "how do I turn it on?" At which point Joseph took the tablet from his dad and turned it on and showed him where to find the files. While Nora was preparing the food Noah went to the church to ask Adam Christus if he could borrow the projector for a meeting he was having in which as there was nothing on for that day so he said "no problem."

Joseph connected the projector to the tablet and the design for how the ark/boat should look when constructed. Also on the tablet was a detailed list of items required which Joseph checked against the list he had created the day before so they could be amended and re-calculated if needed so they would match. On the tablet the first file was a list of things they needed.

- 11,250 4x4x6ft planks of wood
- 310,000 2 inches x 6ft planks of wood
- 4,219 plywood panels
- 144 small windows
- 400 boxes of 100 4inch nails
- 324 boxes of 100 6inch nails
- 500kg epoxy resin
- 50 hammers
- 12 large tubs putty
- 300 rolls loft insulation
11) 100 rolls wire mesh
12) 500 litres cuprinol

After the first file was shown everyone look shocked at the amount of things that were on the list. Joseph then jumped in saying "For that list which is roughly what I wrote down if you give me a couple of minutes

I will just work out a costing based on these figures".

- 11,250 4x4x6ft planks of wood = £7.95 each= £89,437.50
- 310,000 2inchesx 6ft planks of wood = £7.99 each= £2,476,900
- 4219 plywood panels = £16.99 each = £71,680.81
- 144 small windows = £29.99 each = £4,318.56
- 450 boxes of 4 inch nails = £1.74 each = £783
- 324 boxes of 6 inch nails = £199 each = £644.76
- 500kg epoxy resin = £66.00 each = £1,320
- 50 hammers = £4.29 each = £214.50
- 12 Large tubs putty = £3.29 each = £39.48

- 300 rolls loft insulation = £19.99 each = £5,997
11)100 rolls of wire mesh = £19.90 each = £1,990
12) 25 cans of 20 litres of cuprinol = £35.99 = 899.75

Joseph then said the total of all that adds up to a staggering £2,654,225.36 After their jaws had shut properly after seeing the costings that Joseph had done and the shock of it had settled in Noah suggested they took a break and had some food and a drink or two.

When they had all eaten and everyone was back sitting in the living room they carried on with the meeting after much arguing and dirty looks from the wives it was agreed with some trepidation that if they all mortgaged their property along with their savings they would be able to pay for the supplies needed to build the ark/boat. The rest of the cost could be sorted easier as if they go for it themselves by using the haulage Lorries and for a work force split the haulage staff into two teams, they could in fact complete both jobs. Simon looked confused and said "Joseph I know you think you know everything but how can what you just said help?", Joseph said "Its simple half the staff carry on working and making deliveries the other half help make the ark/boat. That way money will still be coming in and to make it fair after a month we swap the teams around." Noah replied "that sounds like everyone is in and Joseph as this is a plan you made maybe you could assist me and project manage the whole build being as though you look like you know what you are doing better than me."

The ladies were sitting there quiet until Hannah jumped in saying, "It's all well and good but where are we storing all these materials" in which Harry piped in and suggested "why can we not move the Lorries from the main building to outside and use that building for storage?" Nora who never speaks at their family meeting said "There is two things you all forgetting about"

- "The food that's left on the dining table
- The food for the workforce as they are building"

"May I make a suggestion you all carry on eating this food so it does not go to waste and I will work on a list of foods that I will be making for you all while the building work is being completed with help from the ladies if I need it? After a few minutes the ladies looked in the direction of Nora then their husband nodded and smiled in agreement. "So as I know there is no objection it looks like Nora's kitchen is a mobile caterer". Everyone smiled and said in a distinctive and loud voice "YES PLEASE." Noah then ended the meeting by saying "Ok if we all agree then the rest of this week we will"

- "Finalize the plans
- Sort the finances
- Empty the main storage
- Move the lorries outside
- Clear area for the ark/boat
- Order the supplies
- Split the workforce"

"Is everyone in agreement?" the men said "Yes" then Noah looked at Hannah, Sharon and Joan saying, "Ladies do you agree as well?" the ladies looked at each other and with an hesitant smile nodded and agreed. Nora smiled happily. At that point Noah gave out a prayer for the Lord for help and guidance and strength for everyone ending the prayer with words from the scripture which was from the talk that started it all off: Philippians 4 v13 *"I can do all things through him who strengthens me"* which sounded perfect.

Joan stood up first and in a kindly manner pointed to where Noah and Nora where sitting and said "STAY" then said to everyone else "Ok let's go. We have a table to clean away and lads the sink for washing dishes in through that door. At that point Sharon jumped in and said "Guys why are you still sitting down? GO."

The strangest thing happened as the dining table was being emptied, Noah and Nora sat down and noticed a magnificent glow surrounding everyone. Nora looked in to Noah's eyes kissed his cheek and said "It will work out just fine."

The week before work started on the ark everyone was very busy getting things organised Simon, Harry and Joseph all went to the bank to see Mr. B Lott the Bank Manager to arrange their mortgage and they were all supposed to state that it was for a big extension and business plans to help them expand. When that was all arranged after quite a few awkward and prying questions from B Lott, the business loan/mortgages were agreed and finalised Joseph and Noah ordered the supplies online by checking the websites to find the best deals to help them to save as much as they could. When everything was ordered Simon, Harry and Hannah jumped in to their lorries to pick up the material and to cut cost they would go for it themselves.

While the three of them were out fetching some of the supplies Noah called a staff meeting to inform the fifty staff about the new arrangement and to see if there was anyone that had any carpentry skills or knew anything about electrical works as that would be helpful to them as well as saving more money from the original budget and on finding out who and what skills they had available. Going through all this would be of great help to Joseph so that he could split the two teams fairly? Unknowing to Noah a couple of the workforce were on the payroll of Jonah and after the staff meeting were straight on their mobiles to arrange a meeting with him. When they met with Jonah they told him all about Noah's plans over a drink and a little female entertainment,

Jonah laughed and thanked the gentlemen telling them to offer their skills to help Noah. Both of the men looked puzzled and said to Jonah "What skills," Jonah stared at them and winked then both men smiled and nodded as they understood what he meant now, but they were to keep Jonah in the know of the building work and progress or wink, wink, lack of.

Jonah at first as the men left was upset as now he had everything that money could buy him as he was filthy rich now, but the one thing that any shop or money could not buy was the love he had been shown from Noah and family and really deep down he did so much miss.

Every now and then although he promised he would never return to that part of the town would drive nearby, hide in a side street and watch Noah and the family and sit back and daydream about what might have been if only he had not met Zach that day. Then a barmaid knocked on the office door for change bringing Jonah back to his senses. When he had looked the barmaid up and down gave her the change he poured himself a drink sat back and was back to his normal self or what he was perceiving as normal. Jonah after that looked up and cheekily smiled saying "Finally Noah has flipped," rubbing his hands saying, "Soon I can buy the haulage yard from Noah and his idiot lads and make even more business using the lorries to fetch and carry under the illusion of a legitimate business with Noah's name on it," At this Jonah gave out a weird laugh. "When I was, younger Noah said that under the company Noah and sons the sons bit included me." After having his five minutes of fun and smiles Jonah went silent about an hour later, Jonah had a big grin on his face made a quick phone call asking the bank manager to come see him,

Chapter 4

The manager a Mr Barry Lott who was a man in his 50's about 5ft 7inches tall his black hair thinning but he scraped it back. He was also slightly overweight but the one thing Jonah knew about that the bank manager was that he had a sick nature and liked young girls, so when the bank manager came to the casino Jonah knew what to do and was waiting in his office. As Mr. Lott entered his face started to sweat as sitting there in Jonah's office was a very young looking Thai lady that was known as Anna. Jonah invited to the meeting on entering the office Jonah pointed Ben to the settee next to the Thai lady, still sweating which in a sick way put a smile on Ben Lott's face but he tried very hard to hide it. Jonah knew different, the young lady was trying to move away as she felt bad at the sight of the sweat of the gentleman sitting next to her, when Jonah knew that Ben was comfortable Jonah then began asking if Simon, Harry and Joseph had been to see him in which he uneasily nodded then Jonah asked what reason did they give for needing the money. After hearing this Jonah laughed and then informed Ben What was the real reason they wanted a mortgage.

Mr. B Lott at first laughed thinking Jonah was making it up but when he realized he was being serious he started to get furious. Ben was getting mad stating and saying "Noah a so called Christian lying to get money I do not believe it", Jonah calmed him down saying "Let the mortgage go through and when it blows up in their face which I have people in place to make sure that it does, I will then pay the loans off for them force them goody two shoes lads of Noah to sell or work for me doing whatever deliveries I want them to do. Then I will get my revenge and then they will owe me and I will be able to get anything I want through the company with me as the overall boss. Mr B Lott said that's alright for you but what's in it for me? What do I get as I need think of the banks money as well"?

Jonah looked with a stare that at first looked like a laser was shooting out of his eyes going right through the bank manager's head. After a few minutes, he looked away smiled then Jonah passed the young lady a small package of what looked like cocaine and gave Ben a key to a private room in the casino. Jonah then looked at Ben then pointed to the door, asking him in a cheeky way what bank money? After that Ben then stood up, grabbed the girls right hand and left. With a dirty grin on his face and a hand on the girl's waist, the girl looked uneasy but kept looking at the packet thinking of how good she would feel afterwards.

Meanwhile on the other side of town after they got a phone call, the haulage yard started to get really busy making space in the main building for all of the supplies for the Ark when it arrived.

The men that were picked to be the first team supervised by Sharon double checked the main building was totally empty and swept clean and no rubbish was left behind just in time as Simon, Harry and Hannah were just arriving through the haulage yard front gates with the first load of the supplies. On hearing the Lorries, Noah and Joseph not far behind them came out of the office with a check list so when the items were unloaded they could pile them in the correct place in the storage in the right order so when building began they were in order to the plans that Joseph and Noah had got for when the building of the Ark started.

Nora arrived at the same time as the Lorries with enough sandwiches to feed an army as well as the men looking right at Simon, at which everyone looked at Nora, then Simon and burst out laughing. Simon when eating was like a bottomless pit. When they had eaten the hard work of unloading began. After Simon, Harry and Hannah had taken a rest and a couple of hours' sleep, Simon, Harry and Hannah were the only ones that could do these trips for the supplies as they needed a company owner to sign for them which made it even more hard work for them but they did not complain. After their rest and they had eaten off they went for a second time.

On Sunday, no one worked but as usual Noah and his family went to church, this Sunday everything was different as usually Noah and his family were greeted and everyone was pleasant but now all they heard was people gossiping and pointing during the service. Pastor Adam Christus mentioned in his talk that God can use everyone in different ways some sound normal things to ask us to do, some are a lot harder and to some non-believers and believers this sounds as if we are crazy.

On the Sunday before they all left Noah, asked Pastor Adam Christus to pray for everyone and their plans to build the ark that they were asked to do in Noah's dream.

At first he was a little overcome about being asked to do this knowing how Noah was a great person for praying, but even people who are great prayerful people even they need prayers as well sometimes even more. On knowing Noah and his family Pastor Adam Christus felt honoured and agreed to pray for them. After he prayed for them he even offered to drop by the haulage company and bless the supplies and pray over the men that were going to be working on it with them if that would be ok.

On Sunday after church the three of them jumped in their lorries to make a third trip for supplies, first thing everyone was at the haulage yard. Harry, Simon and Hannah had returned from their third journey about lunch time Monday just in time to eat which made Simon happy even though all three of them were so tired after eating. While Simon, Harry and Hannah rested the men started to empty the lorries with the last of the wood as this trip carried the wood that was going to be the first that they were going to use,

Just as everyone had arrived Pastor Adam Christus arrived joining them for lunch afterward meeting up with Noah and the family did a small communion with them and after that he walked

around the storage building slightly
shocked at the amount of wood that was
going to be used to build just one
boat/Ark. As he walked around praying
and blessing the supplies. In one right
hand corner of the storage building
Pastor Adam and Noah noticed a large
parcel which was unusual as all boxes
were moved to make space for the
wood that was being used to make the
Ark. On looking closer at the box he
noticed on the top it had written in pen
'Noah and Family God's blessings are
on you all from Mortimer Gage.' On
opening the parcel both the Pastor and
Noah were astonished as it was full of
£1,000 bundles of cash with another
note saying 'for the building of your Ark
God's blessing on you all,' Unknowing to
Noah and his family during the night
after Jonah hearing a voice saying 'you
must stop your angry thought and help
Noah I know there is good still inside
you my child,' Jonah sat and thought for
a while after realizing being mad at
Noah was wrong after all he brought him
up like a son, went to his safe in the

casino office without knowing the exact amount, emptied it all in a box using his old set of keys for the haulage yard. He opened up, turned the alarm off and placed the box in the storage building where the men he had working for him had informed him. Being unsure if Noah would take the money decided to write on it from someone else so he would think it was a donation when they opened up Monday morning. With the assistance from Pastor Adam Christus carrying the box took it to the rest of the family to show them what they found. Joseph emptied the box onto the table in the office and not knowing if deep inside it was enough he counted it and asked if it was ok if Pastor Adam could keep a record while he counted it. After they had finished counting the money with the assistance of Sharon and Joan to the amazement Joseph informed everyone that the amount was two point eight million. Noah showed the Pastor a piece of paper on his clipboard with the cost of the building of the Ark and to their amazement it was the same amount that Noah and his family had loaned from the bank. After what the Pastor had seen he could only look to the heavens and with hands together he called it a miracle. After the money was re-loaded into the box Simon, Harry and Joseph jumped in to Simon's Range Rover and went straight to the bank and gave the box personally to Mr B Lott the Bank Manager.

The second that the money was counted again in front of Mr. Ben Lott and he had written a receipt. Simon, Harry and Joseph had left his office but not the bank. Ben was straight on the phone ringing Jonah to tell him the bad news. Jonah was acting as if he was upset at this stating why he cannot get a break, deep down Jonah was happy when Ben hung up. Jonah walked around his office pacing quicker and quicker until he calmed down. Then he looked up and said, "how can you know how much I had in my safe and I did not".

While they were gone, Noah called all his staff together so that the

Pastor could say a prayer for them while he called the rest of the family together to tell them about the surprise him and Pastor Adam found and the total. On hearing about the box Nora fainted with the shock.

Later that day after Nora had come to Noah stayed with his wife. Joseph who was taking to his Project Manager's position as if he was born to do it passed out the jobs to the men. On the other side of the haulage yard Sharon was handing out the jobs for the workmen that were at the moment still doing their usual jobs and deliveries. The company was still needed to run to bring in money even if it was at half strength. After the drivers had gone out Sharon clipped the office phone to her belt and went to join the men who were on the building crew.

At first the men were talking in small groups wondering how people would think of them building an Ark/boat for a crazy old man and would their friends think they were crazy as well? On hearing the gossip going round Joseph was putting some printed plans up on the big notice board that he and Sharon printed from the emails earlier that morning that were sent on the tablet to the office HP PROBOOK 6560b Laptop that they prepared ready the night before so that everyone could view it instead of first one then other asking silly questions. Joseph stood there acting as if he did not hear them but heard everything that was said. Sharon also heard and texted Joseph as well. She tried to get his attention but Joseph just acted dumb. He was acting as if he was dumb because inside the more he heard the more inside his blood was boiling. Joseph saw the text and replied back "it's ok I can hear what is being said. I will sort it trust me just wait". Sharon was worried as Joseph could not kill a spider in the bath so how can he sort twenty five guys out.

Joseph, when he was finished called everyone together in front of the big notice board explaining why the board was there and where they were to come instead of asking questions unless it was something that was not easy to sort themselves. still hearing them muttering, waited for silence then started by saying a big thanks for offering to help with his Dad's dream like what do I do next and the plan God gave him then suggested that a small prayer would be said before they start. Joseph went quiet, looked up, winked at Sharon, his wife then looked forward noticing his Dad coming slowly into the haulage yard.

Sharon walked over to stand next to her husband, putting her hand on his shoulder, kissed his cheek whispering in his ear "I can see in your eyes you are mad Please calm down it will be fine." Joseph winked and smiled. As Noah got nearer the workforce split to make a walkthrough for him being kind shaking Noah's hand and saying "We are all with you let get this Ark built."

Noah stood near to the building they were using for the wood storage asked if a pray had been said yet to which Joseph said "No not yet, before I let you say a prayer I would like say one more thing if I can." Noah looked at Joseph in a puzzled look and nodded. Sharon knew what Joseph was going to say and moved nearer to Noah, whispered in his ear and said, "Trust Joseph," Noah looked bewildered and pointed to Joseph to speak. Sharon walked up to her husband to give her support.

Joseph cleared his throat. Sharon held her husband's hand as all the workmen who were nearly twice the size of her husband. Before he spoke Simon came from the group of workmen, walked up to Joseph and stood the other side next to Sharon who, while Joseph was clearing his throat whispered to Simon what was wrong in which Simon whispered back telling Sharon to text Hannah, After that he tapped his brother on the shoulder and nodded.

Noah looked again at Joseph who had now calmed down a little raised his arm towards the entrance of the haulage yard and simply said "Everyone thank you for offering your skills, collect your pink slip from Sharon and leave the lot of you," Simon and Noah looked puzzled, Simon knew Joseph was mad at them but did not expect him to be so blunt and straight to the point. Joseph then said "You either leave now and never come back or you can all be quiet and take 1 of 2 offers I have for you all," The workforce looked surprised and started chatting between themselves. While they were chatting Sharon had texted Hannah telling her what Joseph had said and what the workmen were saying and to come back as her services might be required back at the yard very quickly. Joseph had just told twenty five men to pick your their pink slip up and get lost. Hannah at first wet herself laughing then realising Sharon was telling the truth turned up walked as quick as she could and stood next to Joseph simply telling him to do it? The workmen that were in contact with Jonah texted him telling them what Joseph had just said. Jonah read the message and fell off his chair laughing. Joseph asked for quiet then said "My two offers are as followed,

- Admit the uncertainty and your true feeling to my dad your boss Noah and shut up and get on with building the Ark
- Keep complaining while you work and face me and Hannah, Joseph's eyes when he said this looked like lighting"

After saying this Joseph turned, shrugged his shoulders, winked at Hannah who stepped forward to join Joseph without being asked. The workforce that were there knew how strong and angry that Hannah can get. So they found a couple of willing volunteers and walk up to Noah apologised and promised never to complain again. Noah accepted their apologizes winked at Joseph. The rest patted Joseph on the shoulder as Noah said "Let us pray,

Dear Lord,

Thank you for giving us all skills and I pray that every man women and child that his here to help built your Ark that you use your loving arm and surround them

Amen"

After the twenty-five men who were staying behind in the haulage yard to build the boat had thought of what they said earlier Joseph started to walk right through the middle of the men. One of the men at the front, walked to Joseph and said "You scare me now more than Hannah" Everyone smiled as Hannah herself said "Me too." After that to his surprise they all stood to one side rather quickly to let him pass arms raised. While he was passing them some of them clapped giving him a round of applause. When Joseph looked up he noticed something strange as every one of them were smiling and they had a glow surrounding them.

While the men with a new energy within them walked to a storage building where the staff room and canteen was situated which Joseph, Harry and Simon a few days earlier had turned the other rooms nearby in to separate workshops, Joseph and Sharon stayed outside to begin to mark out the area for the ark along with a basic shape of where all the 5ft x 4ft 4inch Squares that the men were now going to make towards building of the framework for the ark.

The twenty-five men that were making the frames looked at the list that was on the new workshops for their name. When inside they saw a detailed plan of the sizes and measurements as well as the amount of 5ft x 4ft 4-inch squares that were to be made with the understanding not to waste any wood. The spare wood from the sides were to be cut into 4 inch pieces and put on the corners at a 45-degree angle to support the Square frames. At first there was a little bit of swearing as the total for the twenty-five men were 4320 squares which meant if Joseph's working out was correct which were most certainly right would mean each man would need to build 172 squares each. After the shock had disappeared the first job which would take them the rest of the morning would be to go into the wood storage building and collect enough wood and nails to begin making the square frames after lunch.

Nora and Joan turned up nearer to lunch time, Nora went straight into the canteen to help start preparing the staff's lunch, Joan had finished her job as an accountant to help with the lunches and where ever else she could assist although at first, she thought that this would not be enough so before she helped Nora and the kitchen staff with the lunches. Noah called her to the office where as soon as she walked in Joan walked straight up to the kettle and made them a drink. Noah accepted the drink asked Joan why she thought she was not doing enough to help with the ark. Joan got herself a drink, started to explain to Noah her problem. Joan said that she felt just being a tea lady was not serving God's dream and she wanted to do a bigger part. Noah, after listening was so upset and replied by saying "If you did not make the drinks everyone would go thirsty and no one could work because they would be dehydrated so in a way if you see being a tea lady is more important than cutting the wood."

Joan left with a spring in her step as well as the same glow that was on the workmen before they started and Joan did a little dance as she walked into the canteen to assist with lunch. When lunch was, ready Nora called Joseph to inform the men to come to the canteen to eat. The surprise was that at first not one man wanted to go for their lunch as they just wanted to work until Joseph said "Ok I will tell my mum no one's hungry." As soon as Joseph turned to leave on hearing that it was Nora in the kitchen they all ran passed Joseph to get there as quick as they could.

After lunch the hard work started so that although they were not all delivering they still needed to keep to the Health and Safety guidelines. Joseph wrote on their sheets that all completed Square frames were required to be stored back into the wood storage building so that he and Sharon could keep a record of them. The twenty-five men were working in two different rooms, both rooms were taking a different way of completing the task of building the square frames.

- In the first room, there were thirteen men and they were making the frames by doing all the different aspects on their own which got the job done but was taking a longer time.
- In the second room were twelve men but before they started they had a meeting deciding to split into four groups of three
  - measuring the wood
  - cutting the wood
  - nailing the wood
  - moving the Square frames to the storage room

After a couple of hours they swapped jobs to give everyone a chance to work and do their part. Joseph noticed how many each room were completing went to visit them and compared them.

That night Joseph and Sharon stayed behind to total up the square frames and to discuss the different ways each room worked together. The next day Joseph left Sharon asleep and decided to go to work early to speak to Simon and Harry before they left for their deliveries, When he got there no one was around which was strange. Joseph went to the canteen to get a cup of coffee and to sneak a bacon and egg sandwich as Sharon had put him on a strict diet.

When Joseph walked from the canteen passing the workshops he heard a noise so he went inside. To his surprise Simon, Harry and not just twenty-five workmen but fifty workmen were busy making frames. The most interesting thing was both rooms were now working in the one place as the folding door which separated them was opened to make the one bigger room. Everyone was following the same system by splitting the workforce so that there were now four groups of thirteen following the same tasks as yesterday.

Joseph nodded to his brother who smiled back at him then Joseph picked up two Square frames that were completed and disappeared into the wood storage. Hannah was in the storage room moving some of the wood around to make more space to hold the square frames as they were coming in quickly and the space was getting smaller. While Hannah was making the necessary space Joseph sat at a desk that he set up in the corner for his laptop so he could do what he did best working on the spreadsheet to keep up with the quantity of Square frames. Joseph had a lot of work as the workforce had now doubled. And it seemed as if the frames being completed had almost tripled.

The new figures read as now that the work was split up into four groups; thirteen per group, the 4,320 frames meant the 332 frames per person would take 111 hrs. so now to complete it would take 2 ½ weeks to finalise the square frames.

Noah and Nora came as usual nearer to lunch time so that Nora could help with preparing the food. Instead of going to the office Noah went to the wood storage building and was doubly surprised by:
 1) The number of frames that were already completed

2) Hannah was there and not doing deliveries. While Noah was talking to Joseph Hannah went inside towards the canteen to get a couple of cups of coffee for Noah and Joseph and while she was there informed Nora that the staff numbers had tripled. When Hannah said the staff had tripled she looked shocked and asked why? Hannah explained that now there will be fifty workmen not twenty-five to which Joan who turned up just behind Hannah had said that it doubled not tripled. Hannah looked at Joan with a hard stare as if she was burning a laser through her to which Joan walked away and hid in the canteen, Hannah carried on by saying "Yes that is doubled Joan but Simon and Harry are here as well, "That comment amused Nora as she smiled and agreed with Hannah's calculations. Joan brought in the coffees for Noah and Joseph as well as a water as Hannah does not drink anything with caffeine in.

The square frames were being made faster than Joseph had worked out as the figures he did were based on them working 8hrs a day five days a week. Joseph had not worked the figures on them turning up on a Saturday as well, so just at the beginning of the second week all of the 4,320 square frames were waiting on the 40 pallets with 108 square frames on each in piles of twenty-seven.

Noah noticing that all the frames were completed, and the staff looked exhausted he called them all together praising all their hard work up to now saying that they can all have two days off to spend with their family and rest as when they get back the main building of the Ark will start.

When the staff had left Noah called Joseph and Sharon in to the office asking Joseph to put his Haulage yard keys and his laptop in the office safe as the two days holiday he gave his staff went double for them. He knew that Joseph would get home and work and while Sharon would prepare the evening meal Joseph would carry on working. Noah looked confused as Joseph handed the keys and laptop right away with no problem or argument and it was all working too smooth as he thought he knew Joseph and Sharon very well. The interesting part was that not having the work's laptop did not stop Joseph at all as he downloaded the files to a usb stick and loaded the information to his laptop at home so he could still work even if he was away from work which amused Sharon as they were both workaholics.

Chapter 5

After the staff had had the two days it was amazing how refreshed they all looked Noah called them together giving Joseph the office keys so he could get his laptop out. Joseph after getting his laptop from the safe winked at his wife Sharon. At that moment, Joseph put his keys into his pocket at the same time as the usb stick fell out, Noah seeing it looked mad and realised why Joseph had handed over his laptop and keys so easily, staring right at Joseph sighed then Noah motioned Joseph and Sharon to sit on the chair that had been brought out. This was strange as doing the talking and giving jobs out was Joseph's job but this time Noah said he had sorted it.

"The twenty-five of you on the left this morning with Simon in charge are to go in the wood storage and make up the Square frames and connect them in a line of nine

The twenty-five of you on the right this morning with Harry in charge are to stay outside and connect the frames in to rows of nine together to make the sides and the base.

Joseph and Sharon if you can keep an eye on the square frames to make sure the bases and sides are the right length

Hannah, can you supervise the moving of the square frames in the rows of nine"

"At that if everyone is happy with their tasks I will leave you to it. After lunch, the two groups of twenty-five to make it fair can swap jobs but not the supervisors." Everyone clapped as Noah left as it had been at least ten years since he had done anything like that before. Noah went straight into the canteen where Nora and Joan were, Noah was in a lot of pain and needed to take some pain killers but the smile on his face in Nora's eyes meant the world to him as he knew he did something which made him feel young again. Noah never left the canteen all-day.

At lunch time the workmen sat down eating away and laughing as the mood on them had completely changed now for some reason they were happy and they really wanted to build the ark.

Noah and his family sat together at a table, Noah asked how the work was going. Everyone was pleased Joseph suggested that when all the parts were completed they painted the wood treatment on when they are smaller rather than when it was fully built. They all agreed. Sharon suggested that the base would be better if it was built in three parts for easy carrying. Hannah smiled wiping her brow then agreed which amused everyone.

The next day all the staff were called in as normal but instead of doing more work on the ark. They were all given invoice sheets for deliveries which to Noah's surprise they all complained. While the workforce were delivering Noah's boys Simon, Harry and Joseph along with Sharon, Hannah and Joan stayed behind to put on safety suits with masks and sprayed the new rows of nine Square frames that were completed the day before. After they sprayed one side they were left outside to dry so after they had eaten their lunch they could spray the other side, not that both sides needed it but to be safe it was done.

The next day the same thing happened. The workforce did some deliveries while Noah's family sprayed the frames. This happened for a week. After the week had finished and everything was sprayed Sharon stopped everyone stating that they had made a mistake, Simon looked puzzled and said "Where?", Sharon said "Give me a minute" in which she got the plans and after showing Joseph he looked worried calling everyone over and showed them that they needed to take 30 square frames out of one of the base pieces as they forgot about how they would move between floors.

The next week the workmen turned up really upset as they thought after all the work they did on making the square frames they had now been forgotten but they were about to be surprised as Joseph was waiting in the Haulage yard and not the office. He called the men in to the yard and when all of them were there he rang Noah who was waiting in the office. When Noah turned up he apologised to them all stating that all he needed last week was just a handful of people to spray the wood ready for today. To the total shock of Noah and his whole family when they said that they would not be delivering but back to building, all of the staff shouted "**YES**" which goes to show how God can work through us all.

The tasks now were going to get harder as now everyone would be outside working. This also made it difficult for Sharon and Joseph to project manage and supervise so to make things easier Noah made the job a lot simpler by enrolling the rest of the family. Noah called the family together to try and give them his support and tell them that he had faith in them all and Noah even picked up a hammer himself and offered his help. Joseph looked at everyone then to his Dad, nodded and made a suggestion which made everyone happy. This was the idea? Joseph asked if Simon and Harry could bring the desk and chair out from the storage building, asking Hannah to bring the notice board and he then had positioned near to the place that the ark was being built. When that was done he asked his Dad to sit down and run the plans and work groups. Joseph then Split Simon, Harry and Hannah to different parts of the build to supervise. Everyone nodded and on seeing Noah sitting there giving those orders everyone including staff and family smiled and again they sang while they worked.

The first job that I want everyone to do is for the fifty of you to split in to two groups of twenty five, the groups will be working as follows; the group next to the storage building with Harry in charge will be the carrying group and the group that looks like they are sunbathing with Simon and Hannah in charge will be working inside. Simon looked puzzled and asked why Harry was in charge on his own and I have Hannah assisting me. As he was saying this he moved behind the workforce to hide but all of the workforce who knew that Hannah was not to be messed with moved to the side showing where Simon was hiding.

Noah commented "Do you question God when he asks you? **NO** so why do you question my orders?" Simon's head lowered Noah continued. Hannah with Simon assisting you will be split into two groups but working as one team. Both Hannah and Simon looked at each other then at Noah who was getting angry now. Noah called Joseph over saying "Deal with them I will talk to Harry's team."

Joseph looked at his Dad and nodded shrugging his shoulders as if to say, "What have I done deserve this," Joseph then gave both Simon and Hannah a dirty look, "Right then what we would like you to do his this.

- Hannah will your group while they are in the rows of nine squares nail the 2inch by six-foot panels of wood to the frames.

- Simon when Hannah's group has nailed the panels on the frames can your group spray the cuprinol wood stain on?"

Hannah nodded Simon looked disappointed but his attitude changed when Joseph said that after lunch the groups will change jobs but sadly not the leaders. Hearing the change of jobs Simon smiled but, when Joseph mentioned but not leaders Simon's face dropped. In the background a small giggle could be heard coming from the part of the storage yard that Hannah was. As all this chatter was going on but no work Noah had told Harry and his team were to take the completed frames and carefully lay them down outside to dry.

That took quite a few days to complete. In fact it was more like over two week. The beginning of the following week, the workforce were split again into three groups. Simon was at last on his own with one group making the base and the other two levels, which his team needed to start first to assist Harry to complete his teams work, Hannah sent out a couple of buckets of 6 inch nails to Simon's team to make sure that they could work in different areas at the same time.

Simon thought hard before his team started as to make the job easier he split his team of sixteen by making them five smaller groups of three asking each smaller team to connect three row of nine together then moving them to one side with the extra person to assist him to connect the bigger pieces to make the three parts of the base to complete one level so that Harry's team could connect the sides while Harry and his group were connecting the sides to the bases. With the bases being made that way it made the job run smoother. Now that the bases were done Harry only broke his team into two groups so that they could work on two sides at the same time. Hannah had the third group and I think she loved this group as she could show off her strength her group was in charge of bringing the square frames from the storage building for the other two groups as well as keeping up with bringing nails for them as required.

Harry asked Joseph to make sure that after Simon's group had completed nine of the fifteen bases that would be required if he would leave the other pieces in the three rows of nine to make the connecting of the left and right sides easier to handle. Joseph looked puzzled as the idea actually came from Harry.

Every so often Joseph and Sharon checked on Noah whist also doing drink runs for the workers as it was getting hot and they did not want them to get dehydrated. After a couple of hours Nora came out with a big smile on her face seeing her husband singing away happy at his desk checking plans. She did not want to disturb him too much so after she brought him a coffee kissing him on the cheek she told him lunch in 1 hour and then she disappeared back to the canteen, Noah then conveyed to

everyone when lunch would be ready
with such style and finesse.

Lunch time was drawing near. Noah,
called his team leaders together
speaking in a deep voice then the next
minute the team leaders disappeared.
Coming back out with paste boards full
to the brim with sandwiches and cakes
which they carried into the storage
building. Joan followed with Joseph
helping with drinks for everyone. When
the tables and drinks were all in the
storage building Noah blew on a whistle
calling lunch. The workforce did not
need a second whistle as they were all
hot and hungry.

While the workforce were eating their
lunch Noah along with Simon, Harry,
Joseph and Sharon walked around the
building work so far and they were
surprised as in the haulage yard there
was the beginning of what looked
something like a boat.

After everyone had rested inside the
wood storage building and eaten their
food the work continued as long as they
could with the weather being so hot and

the fact that it was going dark and unsafe to use hammers in low lighting.

Noah after a few hours in to the afternoon session blew his whistle to stop work, calling the staff altogether to thank them for the hard work said," One final job today and then we can call it a day." Joseph walked up to his Dad then looked at the plans.
Noah saw what he was doing and pointed to the pencil lines that whist the work was being done Noah drew on the plans, the lines he drew were for support beams to be added to the centre at various points to help stabilise the boat. After Noah had finished showing Joseph what he wanted the staff to do, Joseph using the palm of his left hand hit his forehead in bewilderment as he did not think of it. Joseph sent the men inside asking them to make five seventy-five foot poles connecting them together by using dovetail joints and then for extra support hammer nails through the joints. When these were completed they lay them

down flat in the storage yard ready for the next day.

The next day Noah spent the day at the church speaking to Pastor Adam Christus to ask why he has not been to visit. For when he calls Noah turns up but when Noah calls no one wants to know. While he was there Simon, Harry and Joseph with the help from their wives Hannah, Sharon and Joan kept the workers fully nourished and never without refreshments as they worked. The amazing thing was the more of the ark that was getting built the higher and louder the singing got and the quicker the ark was getting completed.

After another two weeks the outside frame work with the support beams now in place was now nearly fully complete, Noah stood there quietly pondering what his workers and his family had done so far, Noah was joined by his family before the workers came in to work that day ready to carry on. Noah asked his family to hold hands while he prayed. *"Dear Lord,*

*I thank you Lord for giving us
the power to do your will and the
strength to carry it out also I pray that if
a few can complete this task you set us
to do what could a world full of people
accomplice if they did it in your name.*

Amen"

As soon as the workers had come in
for work Noah was pleased to greet and
shake all their hands in person which
was unusual as Noah does not do that
normally. When Joseph, Harry and
Simon with their wives walked into the
storage building the desk was again
brought out for Noah. After the
formalities were done Joseph called
everyone over he thanked the workers
turning around seeing his Dad leaning
against the desk Joseph looked towards
Simon looking again at their Dad, Simon
without a word being said helped his
Dad to his seat. Joseph looked at the
plans then asked the drivers who were
now very hard boat builders if they could
add the parts of the boat to each other

to finish the wood making part of the outer hull.

The next couple of weeks were spent connecting the part pieces of the boat together to make the boat complete from the outside. While the outer shell was getting completely finished part of the staff were working in the storage building which was holding the spare wood for they were working on fifty seven foot high by forty five foot wide doors for the entrance as well as working on the ramp to get between the floors of the Ark, and not forgetting the ramp to enter and leave the Ark, After a few weeks of working on putting the smaller parts together to make the Ark outer frame it was finally and totally completed.

Noah had a meeting with his family to discuss the future of the business as they still needed to do deliveries but with the whole workforce working on the Ark no money was coming in to pay wages. It was suggested that they let the workers that were not married to work on doing the deliveries as they could work longer without worrying about family, the workers who were married to carry on with the building of the Ark's interior so that they could spend more time with their family to help with the preparation for when the flood did arrive.

The exterior of the Ark was looked amazing but the harder work on the interior was now needed, adding the two floors to the inside to make spare floors for the animals and Noah's Family.

Simon, Hannah and Harry were sorting the drivers out with work even as the drivers did not want to actually drive anymore. They wanted to stay behind and carry on building the Ark, which was surprising to Simon and Harry but then again not too surprising as they felt the same as the drivers really but they understood bills still needed to be paid.

The rest that were still building were under the supervision of Sharon and Joseph this time though they were basing themselves inside the Ark. Firstly they started by filling in the squares with loft insulation to help keep the boat warm and also to hold the electrical wires that needed to be added for lighting and cooking to stop them from wearing away. After one part of the loft insulation was added and wiring was added a couple of the men started at the far end and began to nail two inch by six foot wood panels.

When the panels completely covered the bottom floor it took them three weeks as they needed to wait for the wiring. Then as the Ark was very big to get the right sizes for the wood panels they kept leaving the Ark to go to the storage building, cut the wood and keep walking back to the Ark.

Noah kept up to date with the progress as he kept sneaking inside the Ark for a sneaky peek and try looking without Joseph noticing but Joseph saw him and because Noah was a creature of habit as well as that he always did the same thing at the exact time daily. Joseph kept an eye on the time and one day hid and when his Dad sneaked inside to look Joseph was waiting to surprise him.

Joseph arranged a surprise for his Dad as the work was complete in the first part of the bottom floor. Joseph arranged that a white leather chair just like the one he had at home to be placed inside the Ark. Noah came to sneak inside one morning Joseph walked behind him saying "got you" after the shock of it Joseph apologised and pointed to the chair. Noah did not get it at first but after a while he just walked over and sat down.

Noah was so comfortable sitting on the leather chair watching the work. He just sat back, made himself comfortable and fell in to a sleep, Sharon ran inside the main building to let Nora know where Noah was so she would not worry. Nora walked to the Ark to see for herself and to tell Noah to let him know he was to stop bothering the workers, Nora walked up to the entrance doors that were now firmly in place with Joseph and Sharon supporting her, walked inside to see for herself. As soon as she got to the entrance way she could already hear Noah inside snoring away. Nora walked straight up to Noah kissing him on his cheek and left.

Joseph instructed the workers to be careful and asked if they could start by putting ladders up against the support beams and against the sides to do the same as the ground floor by starting with some loft insulation. Then wood panels and make the next floor at twenty-five foot higher than the base. To make the next floor it took nearly three months solid work. While all this was going on Simon, Harry and Hannah carried on sorting the drivers. While all this work was being done and Sharon and Joseph were supervising the workers Joan stepped in to keep the office running smoothly.

After the first floor was complete and there was space for the ramp to be added
Joseph split the new group of twenty workers in to two groups of ten.

- This group was to stay on the ground floor to nail panel sheeting on top of the two inch by six foot strips to make the ground floor smoother.

- To bring the wood that was required for the next level to be placed on the panelled floor for easier access.

The work for the drivers was getting less and less so to the drivers pleasure Simon, Harry and Hannah decided to stop giving driving jobs out and ordered them to report to Joseph. The drivers did not query the order in fact they were more ecstatic than disappointed.

The work on the Ark would be done a lot quicker with the full team back on it. While Joseph carried on working higher and finishing the floors, Simon, Harry and the drivers looked at the plans and began making the different compartments for the animals by making wood frames adding wire meshing to the outsides.

When food time came Nora and Joan with Hannah now assisting as before carried on getting the lunch ready and providing drinks.

The first-floor ceiling was finished at almost the same time as the animal enclosures on the ground floor was completed. The family got together to inform Noah who now stayed in the office where it was a little warmer as in the Ark the heating was not connected yet, how far they were doing and also so they as a family could decide what was going on the first floor. After carefully discussing the decision it was decided that the food would be in half with a space in-between and the space at the end would be for overfill for the animals. Joseph, Simon and Harry conveyed this to the workers so while Simon and Harry got to work on the animal enclosure Joseph worked on the other half for the Kitchen and food preparation area and storage.

The second floor was to be Noah's Family sleeping area which would include an area to be enclosed for private areas for a changing of clothes and bathing as all the family would be sleeping in the same area with not much in a way of privacy, Joseph's team was allotted that job while with Hannah helping Simon and Harry's team with the last job that was needed to be done and that was by painting the epoxy resin all over the outside as a waterproofing so when the waters did come along with the loft insulation in-between, the wood would allow the Ark to be warm and water tight.

When everything was completed and the Ark was now built the last couple of jobs could be done and that would be to connect the fridges and to bring the bedding that Noah and his family would be sleeping on. The work was completed but Noah asked all his workforce to still turn up for work the next day which confused the whole family as according to Joan there was no work. Noah filled the rest of the family in on what he wanted when the staff had left afterwards. They all nodded and happily said "Brilliant idea."

The next day all the workforce turned up. The only job to do was to sweep the Ark out and to sweep the storage building so it was clean and tidy. This did not go well with the workforce but at the end of the day they were still getting paid. Lunch time arrived. The workforce walked slowly to the canteen. On walking inside, they were all surprised as Noah and the rest of the family had tricked them. Inside the canteen, a big roast beef dinner for everyone along with champagne and of course a few barrels of lager as a thank you for building the Ark.

Chapter 6

A week had passed and the hard work was now over. Noah and Joseph walked through the completed ark every day to check everything was ok and no gaps could be seen as if they were expecting something to change in twenty-four hours. After about an hour or so they returned and joined the rest of the family that were waiting for them at Noah and Nora's bungalow.

When they returned to the bungalow they were met by a familiar smell but this smell was such a beautiful aroma. Noah looked at the happy smiling face of Joseph. They both went into the dining room and words could not describe their excitement as while they were gone the ladies had not been lazy. On the dining table was a roast beef dinner with all the usual trimmings. There was mash and roast potatoes, carrots and parsnips with a lovely gravy which was everyone's favourite and it smelt so divine.

It did not take all that long to get everyone seated ready to tuck in to their roast dinner. Noah gave a thankful prayer at the beginning before ending with the grace, the whole house suddenly went totally quiet until all the food was gone and the serving dishes were empty. Simon was first to break the silence when he asked "What's for pudding," Nora smiled and said "After you have all eaten you want pudding at which everyone said "**YES**" Nora then said "The usual Apple and Rhubarb Crumble with homemade custard."

After everyone had finished their pudding and Simon being Simon licked the bowl clean as well. A startled Noah and Nora watched as the men stood up and for only the second that Nora could remember they cleared away the dishes. Nora smiled and followed them into the kitchen as she could hear Joseph asking in a loud voice "Where is the washing up liquid kept?" To which Nora stood there laughing. After Nora finally told them where she kept the washing up liquid she turned around still laughing, sat down in the living room where on seeing her laugh all the ladies joined in. After a long while the men came out from the kitchen. They all settled down in the living room and Noah congratulated everyone for the hard work they had done in starting and finally he can say finished on building the ark. Nora jumped in to say "Noah hold up the ark is finished as I think you have forgotten two important things. "The first we can do ourselves and the second is up to God," Harry jumped in and asked his mum what she was talking about as they had finished building the ark. Nora looked angrily right in the eyes of Harry and said "the two things are the animals which are now in God's hands and the one we need to sort is easier and I hope everyone enjoyed the roast dinner we all just ate. It was like our last supper as when this flood and the animals arrive we need sort food out as we have no food left, so unless we sort something out quickly we will all starve and we might have to eat the animals instead of saving them."

On hearing this shock revelation everybody looked at each other with a startled and bewildered look. Simon suggested that everyone should leave, go to their own homes and try in a calm way work out what funds they could muster together for the food in case what was predicted in their dad's dream came true. At which Noah looked at him and glared at him. At this point, everyone looked shocked at what Simon had said after all they had done so far and that it all was correct so far. Hannah calmed everyone down before a huge argument erupted and suggested that everyone met at the ark in the haulage yard the next morning. Before everyone left Noah said a short prayer to help with their discussions.

"Dear Lord,

Thank you for being with us up to now and making your dream you planned for me to come to fruition and at this point I just pray for help and guidance to provide the animals and enough food for the length of the journey you planned.

Amen"

That night while everyone was in their own homes discussing the food and the money that they will need to find, when Noah rang Joseph to ask him to send an email to all their staff thanking them for the hard work and to give them the next day off with pay for a reward.

The next morning after everything Noah and his family had completed all of them had a well-earned lie in till late morning. The first to arrive at the haulage yard was Joseph and his wife Sharon as they wanted to get there early so that Joseph could take measurements to see what space they had for the food that was required and what space was available so that any food that they acquired could be separated for them and the animals.

When Joseph and Sharon arrived at the 'no work 2 hard haulage yard' they were greeted by what anyone else would consider as strange but how things have been in their lives so far, they just looked at each other smiled nodded in acceptance. What they saw outside the haulage yard was a sixteen-wheel lorry with **ALAN AND MICHAEL TEE FOOD SUPPLIERS** written on the side. On seeing this before they did anything else Sharon and Joseph looked at each other and before Joseph could say a word Sharon said, "Ring your Dad first then the rest will not believe this one bit." When Joseph had finished on his mobile they both walked towards the lorry. When they got nearer the lorry doors opened and two gentlemen got out of their carriage walking towards them. On reaching them Joseph introduced himself then his wife stating that their father was on his way. The two gentlemen introduced themselves as Alan and Michael Tee. On first inspection, they did not look like lorry drivers as they were both tall, thin and wore a shirt and tie. Alan was 5foot 11inches with nicely combed back black hair and a moustache, Michael was a little taller but had short dirty blonde hair. They both wore black trousers, white shirt and their ties looked the same which were blue with a mixture of silver and gold crosses, on which matched the shiny name tag which were silver with their names written in gold. While they were introducing themselves, and chatting Noah and the rest of the family arrived in which Joseph introduced them to Alan and Michael.

Michael who preferred to be called Mike said "If we have the right place and after seeing that big boat I believe we do and I believe we are here to help you as you will not understand this as we both at first thought this sounded crazy." Joan who was at the back piped up and said, "Anything you say to us lately sounds normal so please do not worry just carry on."

"Last night while winding down at our local pub the Red Lion in Stoke-on-Trent we were watching the news when the newscaster a Thomas Didymus was reading the news. He was reporting about a crazy family in Northern Wales building a boat which they were calling an Ark and that he doubted that any normal family would ever want to do such a crazy thing. In the other news a Meteor strike was due to hit somewhere in the UK in the next week as if that will ever happen, anyway everyone in the pub was talking about the news both me and Alan who looked at Michael who apologised and said sorry Al just shrugged it off and finished their whisky and went home to bed that night we both dreamt and this is totally weird as we both had the exactly the same dream. After having a couple of hours sleep we both had the same idea went in to work to do what the dream said and here we are."

Hannah spoke next saying "I do not know what is wrong with you both as to us that sounds quite normal," Nora looked at them both then looked at Noah turned to Harry and Simon pointed at their car, turned and said to Al and Mike "You two both look hungry, I will cook some food in the canteen so we can all have a late morning snack. You are very welcome to join us." Simon on hearing the word food punched Harry on the shoulder. The rest of the family very closely followed by Al and Mike went inside the haulage yard and headed to the canteen. Nora waited in the kitchen area for Simon and Harry to behave and then with Joan's assistance cooked the food. With help from Al and Mike the rest of them moved tables together so that they were all seated at one big table which made Noah happy. When the food had been cooked Sharon and Hannah fetched it from the kitchen as Nora was not steady enough to carry it all, Sharon and Hannah along with Joan laid everything in the middle of the table. Everyone's eyes opened wide as there was Bacon, Sausage, Eggs, Black Pudding, Hash browns, Fried Bread and Tomatoes. When Nora came in she was holding the Brown Sauce and Tomato Ketchup. When she sat down Simon asked, "How come as yesterday you said we have no food?" Nora replied by saying "If you must know we have no food at home, the food that was cooked for today's breakfast is on loan from there" pointing at the canteen kitchen. Simon looked at the food then his mum and said, "Thank you" and everyone else agreed. After Simon and Nora went quiet Michael asked, if before the delicious food goes cold, if he could pray and give thanks at which point as Noah always usually prays raised his hand in appreciation and said by all means so when everyone was ready he began

"Dear Lord,

Thank you for everything you are doing in mine and Alan life and using us also we thank you for all you are doing in Noah's family lives as well but most of all I thank you for giving this family the gift of hospitality by making us part of their meal and making us feel welcome.

Amen"

When all the food was eaten and everyone was full Sharon disappeared and when she returned she was carrying a big urn to the table so that while Al and Mike told them why they were brought here they could enjoy a cup of tea or coffee and explain the dream that they both experienced at the same time. Al raised his hand and spoke by saying "As you had said that wonderful meaningful prayer I will tell them the dream we both had."

Al started by telling everyone from where Mike had left off when he said they left their local pub and went home to bed.

" When we got to our homes in which we live about three streets from each other I myself got a drink of water in case I got thirsty in the night had my usual shower then before I got in to bed I did my daily prayers and read a passage from the bible at the moment I am working through the psalms that night I was reading psalms 117 at which point reached out for his bible that was with him as they never left for a journey without taking at least one with them and started to read the psalm

Praise to the Lord all you nations;

Extol him, all you people.
For great is his love towards us,
And his faithfulness of the Lord endures
forever"

".....which was lucky as it's the shortest
with three verses as I was very tired
anyway I dosed off quite quickly after
reading it, that's when the strangest
dream began, the dream was strange as
I could have swore that it was not a
dream as it felt so real. I was standing
outside our warehouse with my keys in
my hand when Mike drew up in his gold
Nissan Juke and parked it next to my
car, got out and asked if I had my keys
which I had. The second we went inside
as if by magic an invoice on a clipboard
appeared in both of our hands with your
address which is farther than we usually
travel but it was in our hands with a list
of item that you required under the box
where the cost should be it said in
*capitals (**PIF**) in which we usually put*
*that when customers (**paid in full**) the*
list was quite a big order and we were
worried that we might need to re-order

stock for our normal customers but this dream and I can say that now was getting more and more stranger. As we took items and added them to a pallet ready to load on the lorry when full, the stock we had on the shelves when we turned to add to the rest of the order seemed to refill on their own after we got the tinned and boxed item, we moved to the butcher's section for the animal foods and the same happened again."

"After that I woke, rang Mike told him and he believed me as he then told me he had the same dream and I should get dressed. He would pick us up in five minutes to go to the warehouse, I kissed my girlfriend got dressed and waited for Mike. When we arrived at our warehouse I looked in the back of our lorry while Mike looked in the front cab, found the delivery note it was just as our dream, that's when we got in and came here." Noah said, "Thank you for telling us your dream and believe me that was not strange or weird it was just God working in mysterious ways." Hannah jumped in and commented that if they have a full lorry should we not thank them and maybe actually empty the lorry. Joseph said "Good idea, you guy start unloading while me and Sharon with the invoice check it off and load it in the correct place on the ark." Everyone agreed with the plan. Nora offered to help Joseph and Sharon.

On reaching the lorry Al opened the back while Mike handed the invoice to Joseph who then ran to the back of the lorry just as it opened. Noah looked inside, fell back as he fainted. Joan caught him nearly fainting herself as inside the lorry it was completely full from the front all the way to the back with food. After the food was being put away in the ark it was getting late so Nora asked Al and Mike if they would like stay to the night at their house and they could leave after breakfast. Before Al could answer Mike said, "If we can have another breakfast like today you got a deal," Nora looked at them both, smiled and said, "Being as it is you I think I can manage that,"

Meanwhile on the other side of East Tridam while everything was going on at the haulage yard, they were having trouble of their own as Police Inspector Saul Hardman was getting calls from all over the town with reports of wild animals like lions, tigers, elephants, and giraffe roaming the streets. Saul could not keep up with all the calls so he popped in to the Casino to see Jonah to get some cocaine to help him cope. While he was there Jonah asked "What is he doing coming in the daytime with his uniform on?" at which as Saul was calming himself down after having a couple of lines told Jonah about the calls he was getting. Jonah listened. After a while he called all of his staff (Hunters) and with the Inspector there, opened a box he had asked his bouncers/hunters to bring in, and handed them all a colt 45 revolver and a Uzi 9mm. He gave them strict instruction to get rid of the animal trouble and not to forget to bring him a few trophies for the office wall. Saul witnessed this but closed his eyes as if he did not know anything which he was a master at doing where Jonah was concerned. Jonah split his hunters up to cover all of the town. After about an hour the first of the hunters while checking the trees in the west side of the town came across two lions who were resting so they called in to let Jonah and Saul know. Jonah looked at Saul and asked, "What's your orders," Jonah knew what to tell them but wanted the Police Inspector to say it to cover himself. Saul was silent for a while, thought about what he heard about Noah's dream, looked up at Jonah who moved his walkie talkie nearer to Saul so they all could hear Saul, then smiled. He said just one word and that was "kill," Jonah then took the walkie talkie, spoke to his men and said, "You heard the inspector." Luke and Matthew the two hunters, on hearing this aimed their Colt 45 revolvers, careful and fired straight at the two lions but there was a slight problem as the guns would not fire so they tried again and again. They would not fire. Luke and Matthew then tried their Uzi 9mm and they too would not fire. This was puzzling them, Jonah contacted them on their walkie talkies asking them "Have they killed the lions?" Reluctantly they said "no" and explained why. Jonah asked them if there was a magazine in the gun which they checked there was. While checking his gun Matthew accidently fired his Colt 45 revolver, the gun this time fired nearly taking his ear off. On hearing the shot the lions jumped up roared and ran away. Jonah was in the casino pacing the floor as he heard the whole thing as Luke was talking to him at the time, Saul just sat there taking another line with Sarah his wife who had decided to join the party. Jonah was so mad he shouted down the walkie talkie telling them to find the lions and next time kill them.

The reports of the animal sighting were increasing so Saul who was still at the casino was stressed out more and more, Jonah was getting stressed as his hunters were reporting animal sightings and every time they reported a sighting

Jonah gave the order to kill them they reported back that the guns did not fire,

The next day work at the 'No Work 2 Hard' Haulage yard started back but when the family arrived all the workers were standing on the opposite side of the road as right outside the Haulage yard were all different types of animals. Hannah who was not scared of anything or anyone walked through the animals, opened the gate and turned around to say, Are you just going stand there or do some work today?" That second the whole of the animals started to move through the gate two by two towards the ark as if they were moving by remote control. The funniest thing ever happened as the animals were moving through the gate one of the elephants pushed in to Hannah knocking her over. On seeing this the rest of the family and the workforce who were all on the opposite side of the road just burst out laughing as hannah was the strongest member of the family and even when there is a fight no one can knock her over but the elephant did the seemingly impossible. Hannah was not very amused at this but after picking herself up, dusting her self-looked at everyone still laughing stared at them all and started to laugh herself.

Chapter 7

After all the trouble of getting the staff in to work when the animals arrived, in the canteen at break and lunch everyone was talking a different tune as when they were asked to build the ark they were talking about how crazy Noah and his family were. Now they are talking about their safety now that there are animal living in a big boat on the same site as they work.

Everything was moving fast for Noah and his family as now the animals were inside the ark they were taking shifts inside the ark so they could keep an eye on them. Joseph and Sharon were working hard in the haulage yard office and listening for the update on this so called Meteor strike that was supposed to hit soon according to what was said by Alan and Michael Tee, Sharon noticed Noah coming towards the door, got up and moved towards the kettle to make a drink. The second Noah entered the office Sharon was standing there

with a cup of black coffee in her hand
ready to hand it to him as he entered.

When Noah entered he had a
puzzling look on his face, Joseph waited
till he sat down and asked "What's
wrong Dad? You have nothing to worry
about me and Sharon have everything
under control." Noah savoured the
aroma of his drink of coffee, took a sip
relaxed back in his office chair, waited a
few minutes. He then asked Joseph if
when Alan and Michael came, did he
notice anything weird. As this was
unusual for Noah to comment like this
Joseph jumped up to get their invoice
that they left behind for them. Joseph
found their invoice looked at Sharon and
his Dad and laughed. While he was still
laughing he passed the invoice to
Sharon who looked at it and she started
to laugh, Noah asked them both to stop
laughing and tell him what was so funny.
Joseph said he would explain but to get
the family together first so that he only
need explain once, Noah agreed, and
they met with the rest of the family at
lunch on the Ark.

Just before everyone was due to meet on the Ark, Thomas Didymus was on the 12 noon news on the television that was set up in the office so that if any updates came through at least 1 person would hear. Tom gave the update on the supposed meteor strike; there was a missile sent to break up the meteor in which it had managed to break it into smaller pieces but there will be some small parts due to hit later that day. The family met in the Ark, Noah slowly walked through the Ark to do his usual check on the animals then joined the rest of the family for lunch. After lunch Joseph said he had some news that both him and Sharon found so funny that they could not work all morning. Noah said finally we can all join in with the joke with a quirky grin on his face. Joseph motioned his hand for Sharon to hand him the invoice and started to explain," When we had the food delivery who can tell me the name of the two men? Simon jumped in without being asked with a smug look on his face and commented, "Alan and

Michael Tee," Joseph nodded and pointed in agreement then he pointed out in this day and age all companies have email addresses right. Everyone looked bemused and Noah said, "Yes but where is the funny thing you were laughing at?" In which Sharon who never talked much at family meeting pointed to Joseph then his seat and said, "Let me explain why we were laughing then we can get some work done this afternoon. "Nora smiled and then clapped, Hannah said "Hurry up then." Sharon said that it was their email that made them laugh. Noah looked and said why is that? their email is almiketeefoods@gmail.com Harry looked at Sharon said "Is that it? That's not funny." Sharon looked around the family noticing smirks coming on everyone's faces except Harry's Nora who was sitting next to Harry clipped him on the back of his head and told him to say the email address quietly in his head and think what has been happening lately. Harry sat there for a few minutes saying the email to himself almiketeefoods@gmail.com after saying it a couple of times a lightning bolt suddenly hit him, almightyfoods@gmail.com the men were from God (Gmail) God's mail company and without noticed started to cry as he was trying to keep the laughter at bay, then he just burst out laughing which started everyone off.

While everyone was trying to stop laughing a big noise was heard coming from outside. Everyone jumped up, went to the entrance to the Ark and then they looked at one another, looked out and saw pieces of the meteor land in East Tridam that was mentioned on the news and it was landing in various locations

Joan took out some binoculars, looked around and screamed. Noah took the binoculars from Joan looked around and saw that the dams had been hit and water was pouring out from them slowly at first but was getting bigger as the strain on the dams grew. Also the mountain on the north side of town, the mountain had collapsed as the Ark was big and they could see all the way round the town. Simon ran into the Ark, got to the top and checked the surrounding areas letting the family know what he saw after which Noah heard all this. He then called all their staff to get on board the ark quickly, but the staff just looked at them saw what was happening and jumped in their cars and drove away. Joan was shouting as everything was going on at the same time saying the workmen were strong but their heart and belief in Lord God that can save them all was weak. Harry on hearing what Joan said nodded in agreement but still tried as hard as he could by shouting after them, to let them know that they should come back and be saved as the road on the south side of town was blocked but they did not listen. They just kept on going

Harry and Joseph went up to their Dad asked him to pray as it looked like the dream he had was now happening. At that exact moment Noah turned around to his family smiled and bowed his head everyone did the same.
"Dear Lord,

Thank you for choosing us for this enormous task and especially for your strength and guidance to allow us to complete this we also thank you for providing us with all our needs but also as you are a almighty God please be with every one of my staff who helped us and put your loving arms around them as they were not fully behind getting on this ark with us in your holy and glorious name.

Amen"

Just as Noah had finished the prayer he looked up and saw Pastor Adam Christus and his wife Evelyn standing at the entrance of the haulage yard. Noah motioned them towards the Ark but they refused so with the help from Simon and Harry, Noah walked up to them, when they reached the Pastor Noah held out his hand shook the pastor's hand and asked him and his wife to hurry up and get on the Ark as the water was slowly covering their feet. Adam looked at Noah and said "No we are both staying in the church, I only came over when I saw the meteors hit and realised your dream was really coming true, and to give you this box of a few things you will need to help you keep your faith as well as to let you all know that I hope and pray as while you were building this Ark I might have prayed over the material with you but I have not been a proper friend, Christian and Pastor."

" I was just like everyone else and ridiculed you instead of believing God and you. I did not believe that the dream you spoke about was real and actually from God. I just thought you had gone mad and I must have given you more work in the church than just one person could manage. When I came to pray over the material I was just doing my role as your pastor and ticking all the boxes and now God's punishment has arrived I must stay with the non-believers." Evelyn then jumped in and said "And I believed you but my place is to stand by my husband, just as Nora and your family stand by you. So I just came to say Good luck and God be with you." After Pastor Adam had finished he and his wife turned around and walked away. While they were turning Noah called out in a loud voice stating how you can be so wrong and so far away from God "Come back and we will pray for God to forgive your sins." Pastor Adam stopped walking and said "I am not deserving of God's forgiveness or yours as I have committed the ultimate sin for a pastor." Noah still mad shouted "You are forgiven in my eyes and God's just come back and get in the Ark and be saved. Pastor Adam removed his dog collar, dropping it to the ground and carried on walking."

Noah was unhappy as he turned around towards the Ark, tears were pouring down his face with so much sadness that he could not walk. Hannah from the Ark seeing how deflated Noah looked ran down towards them telling Simon, Harry and Joseph to go and get ready the big main door while she looked after Noah. Noah looked as the water was getting deeper but when he tried could not go any faster, turning to

Hannah and said "Leave me, look after everyone." Hannah looked at Noah, grabbed the box the Pastor gave him with one hand and Noah's arm with the other lifting him up over her head in what was like a fireman's lift placing him on her big shoulders and started to run towards the big main doors on the Ark where the lads were waiting. When Hannah got Noah inside she turned around looked Noah in the face and said "Are you kidding? Nora would beat me to death if I left you behind," then smiled. Everyone looked at Hannah then Nora and laughed. Hannah was the biggest of them all and Nora would have trouble opening a bag of potatoes without the help of a knife.

The new adventure was about to begin as when they had all calmed down the supports keeping the Ark in place were starting to give way. The waters from the dams were now flowing quicker. As the meteors were falling faster the damage was getting more. As from the top of the Ark where Simon had gone to take one last look over East

Tridam he noticed that the houses were now just rubble and most of the building was just getting to look like piles of bricks. While this was going on at the other side of town Saul and Sarah although they were high on Cocaine they were worried about their two girls Mary and Martha so Jonah called them to come to the casino. When the girls arrived Jonah showed the Hardman's in to his panic room and locked the door After the meteors had stop landing Joseph, Sharon, Hannah, Harry and Joan had joined Simon to survey the damage and also so that they could praise God for keeping them safe and for giving Noah the dream to build the Ark. Hannah and Harry along with Simon lay on top of the Ark to check the sides to see how far the water was rising and if the Ark was holding ok. They knew everything would be fine but just wanted to check. After they had seen enough of what was East Tridam they all went back inside to see how things were.

After the initial shock of the meteor strike just coming out of the blue and the shock of all the family and friends that did not join them on the Ark Noah called his family together to pray.

"Dear Lord God,

Thank you Lord for keeping us safe and giving us the opportunity to build this Ark also we pray for the souls of all the men and their family that helped in building this Ark as well as that can we just pray for the soul of Pastor Adam Christus and his wife Evelyn that your judgement when his time comes to judge them goes on all the good things he has done and not on his unbelief of your dream you sent us Amen"

After the prayer Noah sat down wiping his eyes as he wanted to save everyone but in the end they just did not believe enough that God could save them and this hurt Noah so much.

The work now was not only going to be hard but so difficult as not one of them knew about taking care of wild animals. Luckily for them Joseph, before the Ark building had begun did some internet research on what food each animal would eat and did a cross reference with the food that almiketeefoods@gmail.com had brought. The lists were identical as they knew 'almiketeefoods' was in fact Almighty Foods and that God provides to all who ask:

Lion = Raw Meat
Sumatran Tiger = Raw Meat
Snow Leopard = Raw Meat
Meerkat = Small Animals
White Tailed Sea Eagle = Small Animals
Boa Constrictor = Rodents
Red Panda = Bamboo, Insects and Fruit
Brown Bear = Fruit
Chimpanzee = Fruit, Nuts and Seeds
Brown Lemar = Fruit, Flowers and Leaves
Monkeys = Fruit and Vegetables
Emu = Fruit, Seeds, Plants and Insects
Parrott = Leaves, Nuts, Fruit and Seeds
Elephant = Vegetables
Bactrian Camel = Thorny Dry Plants

Ring Tailed Lemar = Flowers and Herbs
Dove = Seeds
Ostrich = Leaves, Seeds
Giraffe = Leaves
Fallow Deer = Grass, Leaves and
Acorns
Cow = Grass
Goat = Grass
Przewalski Horse = Grass
Sheep = Grass

  To the amazement of Joseph but not
all that surprising when he walked
through the animal enclosures, the
animals had in fact walked to the correct
enclosures. In fact, all the meat eaters
were at one end together and all the fruit
eating animals were all together and so
on. After Noah and the family had got
over the quickness of the dams breaking
and the immediate way that they were
needed to get on board the Ark, they
soon settled down worrying about what
they should do next. Noah who by now
given the amount of time the family took
looking at East Tridam had in fact
calmed himself down and eventually

caught his breath back. Noah called everyone together when they had quietened down. He said with a smug grin on his face that everyone should relax, Joseph who is normally the logical one of them all said," How can we relax with all this still needed to be sorted?" At which point to the total surprise of everyone Noah picked up the tablet that started all this up, typed something into it and feeling proud, smiling to himself, for being actually able to work it without any help, turning it around so everyone can see the file he opened which was "instruction when flood comes" at this point everyone clapped. Joseph looked through the file with Noah and agreed on a plan, the feeding time and clearing the animals mess would be shared equally between everyone, at which point everyone looked at each other nodded and agreed with this. After a while Harry and Simon started to laugh. "What are you guys laughing at." Nora turned hitting them on their backs. She said, "You may be bigger than me, but you are not too old for a good hiding."

which Simon turned saying." What's that for? We were just thinking what fun it would be seeing the ladies muck out the animals while we feed them." Noah then walked over to Nora looked at Joseph and winked. After Joseph nodded Noah showed Nora the schedule for the animals with the times so that the food that she will cook or help prepare, if needed, so that they can coincide, Nora put her glasses on looking at the screen, looked Noah straight in the face and they both wet themselves laughing.

Chapter 8

Harry hit Simon on the shoulder. Both of them smirked saying "Why is it ok for you pair to laugh but not us?" Nora looked at Noah and said "Let me give the jobs out today." Noah would not argue with his wife so he agreed but added the jobs given out today will be for the whole week. Nora cleared her throat and stated the jobs for this week will be as follows:

- Animals food = Hannah and Sharon
- Cleaning animals = Simon, Harry and Joseph
- Adults food = Nora and Joan

Simon looked at Harry who raised a finger as to say something but Joseph jumped in first saying "We did say the jobs should be shared equally and you did both agree Correct?" At this point all the ladies joined Nora and Noah and burst out laughing.

That evening when it was time to feed and empty the animal enclosures for the night everyone was at first nervous as it was the first time any of them had the need to do something like this so Noah called everyone around and prayed
"Dear Lord,

We have done everything to your plan and we thank you for keeping us safe but now can you use and guide us so that we provide and feed the animals and ourselves in a safe manner also can you take the fear from our hearts as we complete this journey and tasks that face us in your glorious name

AMEN"

When the prayer was over Nora looked at everyone and just said "WELL" On hearing that Hannah and Sharon started walking towards the area for preparing the animals food. While they were preparing the animal's food for the night Simon, Harry and Joseph walked towards the animal enclosures to get rid of the waste and sweep where it was needed.

The cleaning out of the animal enclosures was scary but as both Simon and Harry were big men they did not want to show it in front of the Ladies and their brother Joseph, but in fact Simon and Harry were both thinking the same. Both of them were hoping that the other one would clean out the lions and tigers. On seeing this from a distance both Noah and Joseph looked at each other and smiled. Noah who was old and with all the things that had gone on that day was very tired, took the spade from Harry pushing him to one side as he did so. Joseph held his hand out to Simon who gave him the brush, walked right in to the lion enclosure and started to clean. In fact Noah showed them both up even more as when the lion enclosure was cleaned Noah asked Simon if he had his mobile with him. Simon nodded and said "Why?" to which Noah replied. "Pass me your phone and tell me how I can take, I think they call it a selfie?" to which Joseph giggled and

Simon seeing his brother giggle said, "Its ok I will do it." Simon looked at Harry, puzzled as Noah stood near to one of the two lions, Simon took the picture after which they all moved on to the next animal.

Sharon and Hannah were just coming in as they saw Simon and Harry standing outside the lion enclosure with Joseph standing inside and Noah having a picture taken. Seeing this both Hannah and Sharon smiled as while they were preparing the raw meat for the lions and tiger they were nervous, but seeing Simon and Harry standing outside and Noah having a picture standing that close took all their nerves away.

The rest of the cleaning went smoothly as well as the feeding. After they had finished them they all when to the sleeping area and took a shower before coming in to eat. Nora and Joan were just finishing both of them acting as if they knew nothing of what happened. Everyone sat down Noah said grace. Nora asked if they were hungry which was a silly question and then Nora asked Simon and Harry if they wanted beef or chicken to which everyone laughed, except of course Simon and Harry, the rest of the meal went without a word being said.

Over the next few days the food and cleaning of the animals went without a hitch. The surprising thing was every few days Noah and Nora would check on the food to work out how much longer they could remain on the Ark and to a big surprise the food after a full week did not seem to be reducing much. Noah called everyone over and asked if anyone knew what day it was. Joseph shouted "Sunday" to which Nora pointed as if to say **NO SHOUTING.** After that Noah agreed and asked everyone to sit down as although they were on the Ark the church service would still be happening. "Does anyone remember Pastor Adam's gift before he left?" Everyone looked around nodding, Noah moved a cloth that he and Nora prepared earlier to show:

- New international Bible
- Service Book
- Chalice
- Wafers
- Wine

Everyone looked in amazement. Simon spoke first saying "Dad Pastor Adam did still believe in you and God. He just could not make the step in faith and enter the Ark." To which everyone to Simon's reply looked as surprised as it came from him. Noah jumped in saying "So while we are on the Ark Church will still happen and thanks Simon I agree and pray that Pastor Adam and Evelyn are happy now they are with God." Noah asked his family to sit down at the dining table in the eating area of the Ark and started the service.

Today we will start by reading from *1 Kings 17 verses 7-16*

"7. Sometime later the brook dried up because there had been no rain in the land. 8. Then the word of the Lord came to him: 9."go at once to Zarephath of Sidon and stay there. I have commanded a

widow in that place to supply you with food." 10. So he went to Zarephath. When he came to the town gate, a widow was there gathering sticks. He called to her and asked, "Would you bring me a little water in a jar so I may have a drink?" 11. As she was going to get it, he called "And bring me, please, a piece of bread." 12." As surely as the Lord our God lives," she replied, "I don't have any bread – only a handful of flour in a jar and a little oil in a jug. I am gathering a few sticks to take home and make for myself and my son that we may eat it- and die." 13. Elijah said to her, "Don't be afraid. Go home and do as you say. But first make me a small cake of bread from what you have and bring it to me, and then make something for yourself and your son. 14. For this is what the Lord, the God of Israel, says: 'the jar of flour will not be used up and the jug of oil will not run dry until the day the Lord gives rain to the land.' 15. She went away and did as Elijah had told her. So there was food every day for Elijah and for the women and her family. 16. for the jar of flour was not used up and the jug of oil did

not run dry, in keeping with the word of
the Lord spoken by Elijah."
Noah waited for everyone to think about
what was said in the passage.

"Sometimes we get asked to do
things that the Lord tells us to do that at
that moment feels strange. One such
time was when Elijah was told in the
passage I just read to everyone when
he was asked to leave the place he was
in and go to a place called Zarephath.
Although transport was not available in
those days he did not pack any food
because God had told him on entering
the place a widow would provide all his
needs.
So he got up left where he was on
arriving at Zarephath and asked the first
woman he saw who he noticed was
picking sticks for a fire. He walked up
asking "Can I have some water to drink?
Nowadays people would ask for a lot
more but in their time to most people
bread and water was all they ate. As
soon as the women turned to Elijah and
said "surely as the Lord our God lives"
Elijah knew this was who God sent him

to help. The widow continued to say I am picking sticks for a flour as I have only enough oil and flour for one last meal for me and my son then we can die.

Elijah felt for the women's plight but calmed her down pleased God that sent him to do as I asked and make some bread with what you have left. Everything will be ok so she did as she was told and if by magic the flour and oil never lowered so she made some for her and her son and it still did not lower.

How many of us if we were asked to do the same would do it."

After the service was finished Nora gave out the following weeks and their jobs changes

- Animals food = Simon and Harry
- Cleaning Animals = Sharon, Hannah and Joan
- Adults Food = Nora and Joseph

Nora then asked if they were any problems to which Sharon asked "Are you sure? Joseph helping you at home he could burn water" to which Simon and Harry laughed, Nora slapped both Simon and Harry and replied, "You two are probably no better either."

When it was time to start the new schedule at first there was a lot of if's and butts but as they all agreed at the beginning they soon fell quiet. Simon and Harry both looked at each other nodded and even before they started there tasked they tip toed to watch how the ladies coped with cleaning out the animals for the first time to their upmost surprise at first they were hesitant but slowly they started better then the guys did, after a while without their knowledge both Simon and Harry had the surprise of their lives as Noah who was guiding the ladies walked up to where the guys were hiding from one way and Nora was walking the other way, Simon looked at Harry turned towards at first Noah then Nora and at exactly the same time said " We know we are on our way".

Nora followed them while Noah joined the ladies to his surprise the ladies where whistling as they worked so Noah moved away to leave them to it. Nora however had a few words to say to Simon and Harry before giving them the list of foods and what animal was to have what.

While this was going on Joseph decided to show his wife that he can do something right in the kitchen, unbeknown to Sharon he smuggled his iPad on to the Ark loaded the internet via a dongle he purchased just in case the internet in the office failed, downloaded the correct website on how to prepare Vegetables, Nora entered the made up kitchen area was just about to say "sorry for keeping you waiting" before she said a word noticed what Joseph was doing stood there for 5 minutes just watching, Joseph turned saw his mum standing there stopped placed the knife down looking straight at her as if he was a naughty child waiting to be smacked Nora then said " why did you stop by all means carry on" after which she looked over Josephs shoulder asking "what step are you on and where should I start" to this Joseph pointed to the screen and smiled.

When everyone had done their allotted tasks for the day and everyone was sitting down to eat Noah said grace. The food was put in to dishes on the table as they would have when there all sat to eat together. When everyone had filled their plates and was about to eat Nora jumped in saying "enjoy your meal Joseph has cooked it himself" on hearing this everyone sat their mouths open Nora looked at Joseph who was eating raised his head stating "NOT BAD" that night not one word was said while they ate.

The rest of the week went quite slowly there was no service at the beginning of the week and no one mentioned it, Noah was seen less and less that week which worried some of them so on what would be the Saturday night before the schedule change the next day. Simon stayed awake worried then heard footsteps, so he got up went towards where he heard them noticing Noah walking about so Simon crept after his dad. Seeing Noah go down the slope staying back waiting at the top for a while before slowly walking down the slope just enough to see. When he looked he was surprised to see what he saw and that was Noah's chair at the end and Noah walking slowly between the animal pens like a security looking after his place. Noah saw Someone at the top of the slope pointed at them they waved them to him.

Simon came down Noah wanted to know why he was not asleep, so they chatted for a while about how worried they all were not seeing him that much to which Noah explained. "When the jobs were given out that was great everyone was pulling together but after the first week I got bored has I had nothing to do so I lay in bed hearing the animals so I decided give myself a job looking after them while you all rested but when morning came I was so tired I

now sleep most of the day" Simon
replied " you have a job everyday it's to
keep us strong and be our leader our
guidance" all that night they talked
towards morning Hannah woke up not
seeing Simon next to her walked
downstairs to where she heard noises,
when she got there she saw Simon
praying and Noah in his seat fast
asleep, Simon stopped praying looking
at his wife then at Noah smiled, Hannah
smiled back walked up to Noah picking
him up and took him straight to bed.

That morning Simon who was still little
tired led a small prayer session after he
explained why Noah was not always
around in the day. Everyone there
sighed as they never thought that he
was feeling so unwanted. Nora then
decided to join Noah but before she left
gave Simon a kiss on the cheek and the
piece of paper with the following weeks
schedule on which was?

Animal Food = Sharon and Joan
Clean Animals = Simon, Harry and
Joseph

Adult Food = Nora and Hannah

Before everyone went to their tasks
Hannah walked to the sleeping area
tapped Nora on the shoulder and said "I
will do the food today on my own you
stay here" Nora smiled and cuddled up
to Noah.
 Simon who was feeling quite good went
to get the tools for cleaning the animals
when Harry walked up to him and told
him "get some sleep me and Joseph
have got this" Joseph looked at Harry
then Simon "you could beat me up but
you heard him get lost" Simon grinned
raised his hand to hit Joseph but instead
patted him on his head " Yes Bro" then
walked away. The beginning of the
week went quite slowly at first as the
team was down by two people but with
team work and a lot of praying they
managed to cope, half way through the
week Simon re-joined the lads cleaning
the animals out. Nora re-joined Hannah
in the kitchen area to be told by a now
strict and confident Hannah with only a
point towards Nora then a seat, Nora

without saying a word knew what she meant.

 Noah Joined the family at the end of the week looking a lot better and was very cheerful, after having lunch together looking at where they were in regards to the rota smiling to himself prayed and waited for everyone to be quiet, Noah began saying "I know you all have been busy thank you it's amazing how as a team we can accomplice anything as long as we work together" after a few minutes Noah carried on " the next weeks rota is?"

Animal Food = Simon and Joseph
Clean Animals = Sharon, Hannah and Joan
Adult Food = Nora and Harry

On hearing Harry was helping with the adult food his wife Joan sniggered, Nora asked quickly "why snigger Joan that his not fair Sharon made fun of Joseph his food turned out ok" Joan replied "SORRY then came back with Harry takeaways do not deliver to Arks" to which Nora raised her hand and Joan moved away fast almost tripping up.

Everyone went to their areas to prepare when Harry was in the area that was for the adult's kitchen Nora came behind him in a soft voice said "do not let me down try your best" Harry was upset at this thinking his mum thought he was totally useless. Harry keeping his feeling to himself turned to his mum nodded then asked "what we are cooking first" Nora looking worried said "silly question I am cooking a full roast dinner as usual "Nora nearly fell of her seat when Harry said "good can I do the vegetables" Nora nodded slowly. At that moment Noah called for his wife so Nora looked at Harry then added the joint of beef to the oven and left him on his own. Harry had a little secret he kept from everyone and that was while he was on his overnight trips in the lorries he always came back with a couple of wood carved animals to which he told everyone that a customer had done them for him, the truth was he did them himself while he could not sleep.

While Nora was away from the kitchen he peeled the Vegetables and began to carve away at them but instead of cutting the potatoes he attempted to carve a likeness to everyone in each one, the parsnips where boats, and the carrots were animals, After a couple of hours Nora came back without looking at what he had already done said " shall we get the potatoes and vegetables ready now I will peel you can chop" Harry replied " all done now how long do we cook these for?" moving to one side and winking at his mother, on Nora seeing what he had done with them she stepped back nearly falling over but Harry caught her. After the shock she kissed him on the cheek pointing to the chair then said "sit down I will sort it" Joan and Sharon slowly crept to the kitchen and on seeing Harry just sitting there doing nothing looked at each other then whispered "told you he was useless" there whispering was still loud enough for Harry to hear so he told his mum what he heard.

Nora turned looking at where they were trying to hide winked at Harry then said "Joan as you and Sharon are doing nothing you can set the table. Nora and Harry filled the serving trays with the food as Harry was about to take them to the table Nora stopped him on seeing how good they had them covered with foil then let him take them. Nora before the meal started pulled Noah to one side, Noah looked at Harry smiled then said grace, Harry then said before we start I have something to say "the carving that I said were from customers well they weren't "at that point Nora, Noah and Harry removed the foil together to show the food. Everyone just looked in amazement then at Harry. The meal went without any words being spoke. The rest of the week was kind of boring as the food went back to being cut as normal.

The following week rota was about to be read out and to Nora surprise Joan jumped in saying "can Harry cook again" everyone agreed but Joseph said

"although it was brilliant we all agreed
we take it in turn" the next rota was

Animal Food = Joan and Hannah
Clean Animals = Simon, Harry and
Joseph
Adult Food = Nora and Sharon

Sharon started to boast a little by stating
" you had the rest now the best is
cooking" to which on hearing this made
everyone mad, when they were going
towards the kitchen area Nora vented
her frustration by walking near to
Sharon holding on to the door frame
stuck her leg out so Sharon could trip
over it in which she did, has Sharon got
her balance Nora said "you are not the
best at walking let's hope your food his
better" Sharon looked around and said
nothing, Nora had not finished yet when
they got to the kitchen Nora sat on the
seat saying nothing, Sharon turned and
said " what would you like me do" Nora
replied " you said you are the best so
you tell me" Sharon was getting angry
now and in a loud voice said "OK I WILL

DO EVERYTHING" Nora stayed sitting saying nothing. After a while Nora asked Sharon where's the gravy?" Sharon turned around "you do the best gravy" to which Nora replied " you said you will do everything" Sharon nodded then said "ok I was wrong can you help me by doing the gravy" Nora simply looked at her and said "no" this upset Sharon so she stood back took a breathe placed a saucepan on the pan and carried on with cooking the meal, ten minutes later Nora still sitting said "Sharon before you put the saucepan on the stove you did add something to it because I can smell burn" then Sharon turned around grabbing a tea cloth lifting the saucepan up she forgot looking inside and saw nothing but burn without showing Nora opened the porthole window and threw the saucepan out. Nora already knew why she threw it out but still found the need to ask. Sharon without saying anything pleaded with Nora to help and not say anything.

Nora stood up moved Sharon out of the way and started to make the gravy, during the meal Harry said "this meal is ok, but I think my first meal was better" to Harry's surprised Noah jumped in "yours was probably a little better but we do not boast do we" following it up with a hand across his back. Noah then said "his it me or could I smell burning earlier" everyone agreed except Sharon who looked away, to which Nora looking right at Sharon and said " could that be why you threw the saucepan out of the window" Sharon Stared straight at Nora and replied " ok everyone can laugh I said I was the best and I burnt the water for the gravy so I threw a saucepan outside" Joseph then said its ok but hang on isn't it funny you said I was no good in the kitchen as I could burn water and you go and do it yourself" to which everyone looked at Sharon remembering what she said then laughed.

   Sharon for the rest of the week sat on the chair in the kitchen and watched a true master in the kitchen work.

   Noah after the final day of that's weeks rota asked everyone to sit at the table. When there was quite he pulled out the bible and read the whole of the story of Noah's Ark when he reached the part where it said for 40 days they were on the ark he stopped picked up a piece of paper looked at it and said " so far we have been on here for thirty five days so if we are going by the bible story of Noah's Ark that has served us well up to now this will be the final rota we so I am adding an extra job to the list.

Animal Food = Joseph and Harry
Clean Animals = Sharon and Joan
Adult Food = Nora and Simon
Water Level = Noah and Hannah
Noah continued "I have put Hannah with me but after our checks Hannah can you help with cleaning the animals" Hannah just nodded, Nora looked funny ay Hannah and said "your turn complain about my son" Hannah looked at Nora then Simon and replied " I have two reasons why I not said anything 1. If you can get Harry and Joseph cook carry on and 2. If he makes me look bad I will

sort him myself" Simon gulped, Simon walked to the kitchen talking real low asked his mother "what do you want me to do" Nora pointed to the Vegetables and said "you eat enough of them to know how small they need be so start there. While this was going on Sharon and Joan were cleaning away all of a sudden Sharon was talking to herself, Joan asked her what's wrong to which Sharon said " I cannot forget burning water I have even been having dreams about it" Joan smiled and replied to her " try not think about it think about this instead we now know both our husbands can cook" Sharon smiled and instead of talking to herself was now whistling away.

Noah and Hannah would check the water levels twice a day once in a morning and once at night by wearing a miner's torchlight on their heads and picking a point in the distance, the beginning of the week the levels still looked the same, towards the middle of the week the Ark seemed to rock more and more so Noah and Hannah checked more than twice a day.

Chapter 9

Now the ark seemed to start to lower
Noah asked his sons along with Hannah
to check outside. When Simon and
Harry and Joseph tried to straddle by
opening the main double door to check
on where the flood was Hannah stood
still for a few minutes in what looked like
he was in a world of his own, then
suddenly walked over to one of the
windows looked out taking a certain
point in his eye line studied it and
noticed the water levels were indeed
lowering. Hannah then walked over to
Noah telling him the waters had indeed
started to lower in the same time as it
took his brother to open the main doors,
Joseph walked over to them and told
them the waters were lowering. He
passed a message from their dad to re-
shut the door at which point after wiping
the sweat from their heads cursed under
their breath then started to shut the
Ark's main doors.

Noah called the family together and
informed the ladies of the finding that

the lads had found out about the waters. Sharon got the calendar that she brought from home and counted the days that they were in the ark. It was **40 DAYS.**

The flood waters started to lower more quickly towards the end of that day all of a sudden the ark stopped and started to rock a little. Noah knew that the sudden stop must be that the Ark had landed and outside as the flood had nearly disappeared so again Noah asked his sons with their wives help this time to open the main doors. On opening the main doors at first they looked around to try and get their bearings as all they at first could see was demolished and derelict property. When they did find out where they landed they looked at each other then looked to the heaven and laughed and laughed at which point Noah and Nora joined them asking what the laughter was about. Harry pointed outside for Noah to see and he too started to laugh, after they all laughed for a while Sharon said to Noah "Please tell me why we have landed on the back of the **Arrow** Hat **Casino?**" Noah gave out a thankful prayer.

"Dear Lord,

> *Thank you for keeping us safe during these 40 days and I know you know everything that is to happen in our lives and you have an ultimate plan for each of us, please show us the reason why you have landed your ark here your holy and majestic name. AMEN"*

After Noah had finished the prayer they all said amen. Simon, Harry and Hannah walked out first slowly so they could make a path through the rubble. While they were making the path the rest of the family started to open the animal enclosures and they were all totally surprised and shocked as the animals were waiting 2x2 for their enclosures to open. As soon as Noah and his family opened them the animals walked out side by side just as the animals entered. The animals walked down the uneven but kind of straight path that Simon, Harry and Hannah had made as soon as they found a normal if you can say normal in an area full of demolished and broken down buildings, the animals dispersed and went their separate ways. Simon, Harry and Hannah went back into the Ark to rejoin the family.

After the animals had gone from their sight Noah and Nora had one final walked around the ark to do one last check for any animals left then as a family unit they all stood together in the entrance to the ark and just stood there silent.

What seemed like only a few seconds turned out to be almost 1 hour later when Joan shouted "**LISTEN I CAN HEAR SINGING**" after everyone had got over the shock as Joan was not known for shouting in fact she had quite a low voice. Noah listened hard and agreeing that there was a sound coming from somewhere asked the lads Simon, Harry and Joseph along with their wives Hannah, Joan and Sharon to take a separate area to see which one could hear the sound of singing the loudest, so they knew where to dig and look more to check for survivors if in fact there were any.

After quite a long time, about three hours later as soon as night fell and the dark black skies were starting to appear, Sharon shouted out, "Its coming from over here" On hearing the shouting everyone came running with Noah and Nora taking their time by walking slowly as their balance was not perfect and their old age, but on seeing them walking slowly Hannah rushed over towards Noah and Nora putting her arms under them so they could use her strength for assistance with their balance on the last little bit, as they were walking in the direction of where the sound of singing was coming from, Noah tried to walk quicker but stumbled so Hannah took a better hold under both Noah and Nora and was literally nearly carrying them both.

When Hannah and Noah with Nora got there Simon and Harry together with Joseph told them what to move so when

they were moving stones and rubble
they did it in a safe and proper way. As
the darkness was falling while Simon
and Harry were moving the materials
away Sharon and Joan were standing
there holding torches.

The place where they were moving
material was the other side of the casino
to where the ark had landed. The more
they moved the higher the singing was
and after quite a long time they started
to see what looked like a doorway.
Simon and Harry with Hannah's strong
arms cleared a path which with Joseph
on one side of him Noah walked up to
the door, knocked on and asked how
many were left in there and to their
surprise heard a voice that they thought
they would never hear again. Jonah on
hearing Noah's voice shouted out
"PRAISE GOD IT'S YOU THANK YOU"
Then after a while Jonah said, "Sorry
there are five of us, myself and the
Hardman family",

Noah asked Jonah if he could open
the door in which he replied, "I wish I
could the lock is broken", Hannah who

had walked towards Noah to help stabilize him shouted to Jonah "MOVE AWAY FROM THE DOOR" After 5mins Hannah using all her might pushed on the door and with all her strength as from the whole of the family she was stronger than Simon and Harry put together, after two attempts the door gave way all five of them inside the panic room which is where they all hide before the meteors strike, all of them were barely standing but as soon as the door was kindly opened from nowhere they found strength from somewhere. They all came out. Saul and Sarah were helped out by their daughters Mary and Martha because they for some reason looked a little worse for wear. Although for one weird minute the glow that surrounded the girls was almost blinding. Jonah on the other hand although at first his standing was a little weak, when he came out of the panic room emerged with what looked like skipping and his white suit although a little dirty shone as if he was covered in diamonds.

When Sarah and Saul had got out and
a little away from the rubble, although
they looked a little worse for wear, Saul
found enough strength to lift his arm and
give a big hard hug to Noah that his face
was turning red. While his arms were
still around Noah everyone was shocked
to hear coming from his mouth as Saul
had always laughed at Noah and his
family every Sunday as he saw them
leaving the church, Saul said in a high
voice "PRAISE BE TO THE LORD GOD
ALMIGHTY I'M SAVED" Later when
everyone had taken in what Saul had
said Jonah was nearly in tears has he
walked with Noah away from the rest of
his family to ask if any more people had
been found dead or alive. In which Noah
replied that "You at the moment are the
only ones we found due to the fact when
they landed in the back end of the
Casino and the only sound they could
hear was from the singing that you and
the Hardman's were making."

Everyone went to the ark to keep
warm with help from the others for Saul,
Sarah and Noah and Nora as it was

dark now and their balance was not that good, the main thing though was which put a big smile on Noah and Nora's face was that everyone was singing praise to God as they all walked. The kitchen area in the ark was not that big so Simon and Harry broke wood from some on the enclosures and made some makeshift seats. Nora looked to see what food was left so she could feed everyone, while looking in the store cupboard to see what was there Jonah walked behind her and asked if she wanted any help. On seeing what was there he then walked out of the kitchen area stating that he would be back in a minute, in that minute that Jonah was gone he called Simon and Hannah over handing Simon a key saying, "Be careful as you go and in the back of the panic room there is a door to a small room in that room is a few cupboards, open them and bring what is in there," Hannah looked at Jonah in a discussing way then looked at Noah who looked at Jonah who winked and said "I'm going help Ma oh sorry Nora," Nora hearing him call her Ma shouted in and said "THAT'S OK SON" in which Jonah smiled while wiping his eye. Noah looked at Simon and said "You still here?"

When Simon and Hannah got to the place they slowly walked inside using the torches that they had looked around and found the door that Jonah was talking about. Simon tried to open the door but the lock seemed to be stiff so Hannah pushed him aside, winked then grabbed the door handle and amazingly the handle came away in her hands. Simon opened the door slightly, shining the torch inside to check if it was safe and seeing what was inside he swore, closed the door and walked away, As he walked away Hannah slapped the back of his head for swearing and asked what was up. Simon pointed at the door. Hannah looked inside swore, herself, turned to Simon and said "Don't you dare."

After a while of cursing and swearing Simon and Hannah opened the door fully to reveal a whole room full from top to bottom in every kind of food both basic and posh with a separate generator which when the door opened the light came on. As they had been gone for a while Sharon, Joseph and Joan along with Harry came to the panic room shouting "Is everything ok?" Hannah shouted "YES GET IN HERE" When everyone was inside Simon opened the door wide so that everyone could see inside the room. After even more swearing and cursing then eventually when the shock had gone Joseph said, "Why are we standing here? let's take this all to the ark." As soon as the boxes of food were nearly at the ark Noah and Nora with Jonah were standing at the entrance when the lads along with their wives were in view, Jonah kissed Nora on the cheek. "Can you make use of this Ma?" then turned to Noah and said "I'm sorry Dad."

After the boxes were inside the ark and Nora looked through them she cooked a feast for everyone that was fit for royalty with the assistance from Mary and Martha. Before the food was served

Noah looked up and Saul asked if he could give thanks and say grace before they ate. Noah with a shocked look on his face agreed. While the food was being enjoyed Saul looked at Sarah, nodded and she asked if after the food was over and with her and Saul's help to tidy up, can they please tell everyone what happened to them in the panic room while the meteor struck and the flood that destroyed East Tridam.

Sarah looked at Noah and Nora winked then hit her husband Saul softly on the shoulder in which he took the hint and started to collect the dishes, and without asking Jonah, jumped up and assisted in collecting the dishes. When they got to the makeshift kitchen in the ark Jonah and Saul started to argue but the subject of the arguing made Sarah laugh as Saul and Jonah were arguing over who was to wash and who was to dry. On hearing the laughter everyone came towards the kitchen area, saw what she was laughing at and joined in which at that point Saul and Jonah stopped arguing. Nora came in as the voice of reason hitting them both as if they were being naughty school children and suggested they took turns washing and drying the dishes.

The dishes and plates were all clean and put away when Jonah went into a box that was not opened, looked inside and pulled out two bottles of Penderyn Welsh malt whiskey, asking if anyone wanted to join him in which everyone raised their hands. Also, he pulled out a bottle of non-alcoholic wine for Mary and Martha as they were underage.

It was finally time and Noah were indeed very interested in listening to how being trapped inside a panic room had changed the way that Jonah and the Hardman's saw things so dramatically. Saul took a drink then said, first before I start I would like to thank and apologise to my lovely daughters."

Mary and Martha smiled, Saul started "Noah you were totally right not to trust me as I was the Inspector I thought I could be beyond the law but I was wrong. Sarah held her husband's hand as he continued.

"Sarah and I were a young couple before the girls arrived. We were always going out and on one occasion Sarah was at a party alone as I was busy. She had drunk a little so a friend of hers offered her to try Cocaine to help the party go better for her. So she took a line. At the next party it did not take Sarah long to find her friend and ask her for another line. At this party I went with her and after Sarah took a couple of lines said I was a kill joy if I did not take one line, so under pressure I took a line and just like everyone else who only tried one line it was never enough as you get a buzz from it. Every party after that we would take some cocaine with us and join the rest getting high, after a few years and the girls arrived we moved here. I got a promotion to Inspector and every so often we took trips to London to buy our supply but it was costing more and more as we were both getting hooked. Some days before we got the girls up for school we would have a few lines before we got out of bed. The one good thing was and even if we were in deep need we never took cocaine in front of the girls, Getting back to now? Jonah was our new supplier but since the casino opened I started to gamble to pay for the cocaine so when Jonah paid me to look away I would gamble it away but still required the cocaine."

"Jonah decided to pay the debt I owed. He would take our daughters for his other business, so I came to try and stop him but on my way to the casino I needed Jonah's help with a few lines of Cocaine to help me cope with all the animal calls coming in, the real reason I was going there. All I could think about was more cocaine and I now know my girls are more important than anything. Sarah joined us to support me in telling Jonah not to use the girls as payment, we will find the money we owe but firstly as soon as Sarah saw the cocaine that was it then we heard about the meteor strike, and that was how we came to all be in the panic room in the casino. However the door automatically locked when the meteors hit the town.

Jonah rang Mary and Martha to come to the casino as both me and Sarah were there and as they were good girls, without question they came right away in which after the meteor hit I am so glad they did."

"The main problem was Jonah had his drugs in a safe place in his office and none in the panic room. Sarah and I along with Mary and Martha were locked in here desperate for some cocaine so I am deeply sorry girl's that you saw us in that state, to which the girls both together said "Its ok you were both unwell we still love both of you."

"When we had been in there for about a day both me and Sarah started to sweat and shake without them knowing why our girls wiped our brows and cuddled up to us taking care of us when we were feeling unwell. However we got worse by shouting out for no reason, feeling tired and being quite agitated and always being so restless. Our energy was failing us but we kept on trying to move around. Whenever we did finally get to sleep, after we got comfortable, our dreams were not very nice. In fact some of them were so scary we would lash out and scream."

Martha jumped in," Its ok we now know what you were going through. If I can continue for you? When me and Mary were trying to calm you down during your bad dreams. Mr. Whey here explained what you were in need of and has you had not taken any cocaine for ages, as well as explaining what cocaine was, and how the drug when you take it can give you a false sense of reality that you can handle anything while taking it as well as that the thing you were going through was something called cold turkey." When Martha took a breath and was gaining her composure Jonah was by her side saying. "It's ok and by the way call me Jonah not Mr Whey," Martha smiled then continued." While you were sleeping both me and Mary who was looking after her mum and I was looking after dad, we were both tired so after we had calmed you both down and were fast asleep Jonah offered to keep an eye out while both of us slept."

Saul and Sarah hugged their daughters and started to cry for what they had gone through because of them and their foolishness. Jonah then said, "While they were all asleep I just sat there looking at them, looked up and then found myself praying to God, *"Thank you God for keeping us safe even though I do not know why you have saved us and there are better people in the world than what I have done, thank you Lord for these girls who have gotten the strength to just help their parents when they needed them, please Lord help me to help them in your strength and almighty power. AMEN."*

"After a few hours Saul at first woke with a fright as he was having a bad experience in his sleep then Sarah woke so I tried to keep them quiet as I was pointing to the daughters who were so tired they feel asleep standing up resting against the wall. "Saul said "Please tell me you were not praying as you do know their is no God. At that point I just looked at him and said "Who you think gave them two girls the strength to look after you?" Sarah hit Saul behind the head weakly then said "It sounds daft and weird but I do actually believe that." Sarah started to pray as well but her prayer was all over the place so she asked me if I could teach her how to pray. Saul looked at us both and said, "Can you teach me as well?" The girls were still asleep and to me it looked weird but to you Noah it was normal but the three of us were kneeling on the floor praying to God for him to find it in his heart to save us."

"When we looked up I noticed the clock and we had been praying for seven hours, Mary and Martha had woke up and without us knowing had knelt down and were behind their parents praying silently as well. I stood up and pulled my sunglasses from the inside pocket of my suit as the light coming from Mary and Martha was so bright. Sarah and Saul both stood up looked at their daughter lifted them up in their arms hugged them and Saul SCREAMED "I BELIEVE IN YOU GOD THANK YOU" We all stood there and hugged with me helping the girls support their parents and started to sing. That's when you knocked on the door."

After hearing all this all of Noah's family the lads and their wives all were crying but they were crying tears of happiness .Noah thanked them all and suggested that they found a corner and tried to get some sleep and we can all talk about the next move in the morning.

Late the next morning Noah and his sons Simon, Harry and Joseph as well as Jonah were all up and making plans, while for a change for Nora, Sarah was cooking the breakfast. The plans that they were discussing were how to split the town up so a proper and full search could be carried out now it was light.

Noah = Stay behind with Joseph at base and co-ordinate
Simon & Hannah = North of town
Harry & Joan = East of town

Jonah & Sharon =   South of town/check
entry to town
Saul & Sarah = West of town
Nora with Martha & Mary = clear
breakfast and prepare sandwiches for
lunch

Noah suggested and everyone agreed
to call in every two hours or if they find
something. After 30 minutes Joan rang
base camp to let them know that the
road that was at the south of the town
was completely blocked but Jonah was
trying to climb it to see how bad the
blockage was and if it was movable. The
rest of the search team called in after
two hours to report only dead bodies but
they would keep looking longer. Noah,
when Simon rang in, told them what
Joan had said and asked if they could
go to the South side and see if they
could help.

When Simon and Hannah had
reached Sharon she was pacing around
as it was ages since she heard from
Jonah. Hannah looked at the blockage
and Started to climb, turned round and

said "I will go check on where he is. Pass me your phone Simon. I will ring Sharon when I see Jonah." After 25 minutes Hannah rang to say not to worry Jonah is safe. "We will be back soon, go to the ark base camp we will meet you there.".

Sharon and Simon went back to the base to find everyone there. Harry jumped up. "What is the good news then? Hannah rang us saying get back to the ark. I have great news" Sharon looked at Simon, shrugged her shoulders and said "I do not know". Joseph was on his phone, walked in and said, "Hannah and the rest will be here soon. They will explain."

Hannah and Jonah walked in after one hour laughing. Jonah said, "Ma put kettle on. We have guests, Hannah moved to one side to reveal about twenty emergency service people and volunteers."

Nora looked at Jonah, Smiled and said "Well come in then," The Head Emergency Man said that they had been on emergency alert looking for survivors

since it started but found nothing then
the helicopter that was flying overhead
noticed a big boat and the waters going
down "We thought we would try one last
place as we tried to get in. We then saw
this gentleman climbing over so we
made a path through the blockage and
here we are." Jonah being the
gentleman said, "While you are waiting
for the kettle would anyone like a malt
whiskey?" A few of them said yes.

While the volunteers were having a
cuppa and some sandwiches, Joseph
and Noah were back to work trying to
work out what they were going to do in
regards to starting a re-build of the town.
While they were away from the group a
number of the volunteers were chatting
with Simon and Harry about what they
did for a living when they were not
volunteering. Harry called Noah and
Joseph over and in a kind of rude way
told his dad to bring his tablet. Noah
was surprised at what he heard. The
people that volunteered were not only
there to look for survivors but to help

and advice with the re-build or makeover of any town that needed help.

Jonah pulled Noah away asking if he could talk with him. On seeing them move away Saul went to join them. Both Jonah and Saul seemed to want to say near enough the same thing. Saul started by asking if Noah could forgive him for bad mouthing him for being a believer and for going to church and also when they re-build would him and his family be welcome to join them. Noah smiled and said "God has forgiven you already. That is why he chose to save you so why should I judge things that are in the past. The church is always open to everyone." Saul walked back to Sarah and they talked about what Noah had said to him.

Jonah said "That's nice what you said to Saul but you must not be able to forgive me for I insulted you and your family after you helped me when I was in need, plus all the bad things I did to you and your family." Noah looked at Jonah and said "How can I be mad when Mortimer Gage is you, the mystery person who paid for the Ark". Jonah looked surprised saying "Who me?" Noah walked over staring Jonah in the face and said "yes you. The alarm key code is a special one I gave you." Jonah replied "I was trying to ruin you. Why would I do something like that?" then winked at Noah. Noah was getting mad but paced a little and said. "Jonah there is a story in the bible that Jesus told in a parable about a son who wanted to be a man and leave home but when he was in need he came back to his father who welcomed him back." Jonah was confused. At that point Simon, Harry and Joseph walked over. Joseph and Simon put their arms around Jonah while Harry who had a piece of cake in his hand stood next to his dad and said what my dad was trying to say was **WELCOME HOME**." Jonah was nearly in tears and said "Thank you but I'm no good and I did wrong." Noah smiled commenting on what he said to Saul and then he said "God has forgiven you and so have we. Your good deeds by providing help for Martha and Mary and supplying the food them count. I suppose they are just like your Act of Random Kindness." Jonah still looked confused as Noah and the lads walked away smiling at which Joan and Nora who were starting to tidy away said "What is wrong?" Noah replied "Nothing just a family bit of humour."

Chapter 10

When all the trees and boulders were, all cleared away and the dead bodies of the town folk buried, the whole of East Tridam was empty apart from a rundown building that was erected and made liveable for Noah and Saul's family to live in.

A plan was formed and a protype blueprint of sorts was created on how the new East Tridam was going to look. As the last of the rubble and people were leaving Jonah and Saul's Family left with them carrying the made-up blueprint to try and show it around to try to sort out some funding to re-build the town back to how it was. Unknowing to Noah and Saul, Jonah knew where to get enough funds to build the town maybe even enough to build a better town.

As they were leaving Jonah along with Saul and his family as there was not much for Saul to do so he decided to treat his daughters for helping them when they needed it so they all joined everyone in thanking the numerous helpers that came to help removed everything. On arriving in West Tridam Jonah went straight to his Financial Advisor/Banker, Saul and Sarah went to the uk deed poll office has while they treated their daughters to a shopping trip on their own, they in fact now that they are starting afresh with God they both decided to change their names, after a couple of hours they reintroduced them with their new names Paul and Paula Hardman. Although Jonah had Ben Lott in East Tridam in his pocket he did not trust him with the funds he acquired from his illegal activities. The Financial Advisor Jonah used was a Mr. Nicholas De-Most also Nicholas De-most did not ask where Jonah got his money from as long as his percentage was sufficient. At first Nicholas was very happy to see Jonah after what he heard about the meteor strike but after hearing Jonah's story and the plans he wanted to do he was not so happy. Nicholas had made a few plans of his own with the money. Over the next 3 years he could buy West Tridam United Football Club his favourite team.

Nicholas typed Jonah's account details in the computer so that Jonah could see them, Jonah at first was standing behind Nicholas but after seeing the amount he had fell straight back as he was in shock. When he noticed in the account he had amassed the total of two billion pounds. When the shock had subsided Nicholas's secretary brought both Nicholas and Jonah a Malt whisky. Nicholas at first just put his on the desk but soon drank it after Jonah told him he was shutting the account "This is what I want."

- "First billion is to be moved to my person account
- Second billion is to go to a charity. You can set up an account to compensate all the families that lost loved ones in the meteor attack
- To make it fairly handed out I am appointing Joseph, Noah's son as Executive

- After it's all done you are no longer required as I have changed."

After seeing his advisor Jonah rang Joseph swearing him to keep all he is doing a secret until he arrives back in town to which Joseph agreed.

While Jonah was away he made a few phone calls to certain people he thought would be able to help. Starting with suppliers of building materials and road workers. But before that he contacted Red Dragon Architects to arrange proper plans and a more detailed blue print to be made. Two months later Jonah met up with Paul Hardman and family then contacted everyone to arrange that they all entered East Tridam together. Everybody gathered on the outskirts of town until Jonah arrived. When Jonah arrived Alan and Michael Tee introduced themselves to him to ask if he thought Noah would like this pointing to two 16 wheel lorries with Noah's firm's name written on the side, Jonah had tears in his eyes and just saluted after which Jonah jumped in the first vehicle and smiled then said "Wagons roll"

Simon was doing a walk around the empty site as since Jonah left everyone was doing it in turn. All of a sudden Simon noticed a vehicle coming into town. He picked up his binoculars, seeing Jonah waving, Simon grabbed his phone and rang his Dad who told everyone else. When the vehicles were all parked up everyone had arrived to see.

Jonah with Alan and Michael Tee walked up to Noah who was now getting very frail. "Before we start unloading, Jonah asked Noah if he could follow Alan and Michael as they have a small gift for you." Noah with Hannah nearly carrying him followed with the rest not far behind. Saul who was now Paul walked up to Noah showing him their new names and also seeing the Lorries Noah started to cry. Simon and Harry stood there with their mouths open but no words would come out which surprised everyone. After the tears had almost stopped flowing Alan opened the back of the first lorry and inside there was more as fastened in the back was a statue of three dams. Michael explained that "In the van behind us are three stone masons. If you give them the names of everyone that died they will add them to it so a memory can be done and placed in the middle of town for years to come. Now everyone was speechless until Nora shouted "Kettles on who wants a drink?"

   The next morning Jonah introduced Noah to Glenn Ables from Red Dragon Architects along with his assistant Leo Ross, who had drawn up the plans and also offered to stay until the new East Tridam was built. At first Paula looked at her husband Paul then at Leo and said to herself "NO".

Paula walked up to Leo and said " you look like my husband you are not related are you" Leo replied sharply " I do not know my mum died giving birth to me all I have his a photo of them together"

Paul came over not knowing about their conversation looked at the photo and asked Leo " why have you got a picture of Ruth Harmony and myself at college" Leo looked shocked and walked away, Paula pulled Paul to one side and said "we can talk later Leo was holding a photo of his dead mother and his father" Paul looked at his feet then after a while looked up and said to his wife "I am sorry but I think I need speak to Leo 1st" Paula agreed. Unbeknown to what had gone on.

Harry popped up and said, "That's all well and good but have you managed to get enough funds to build a new East Tridam?" to which Joseph hit him on back on the head, winked at Noah and Jonah and said, "All funds are sorted, A mystery person has donated just enough to cover everything." Noah looked at Joseph then Jonah and smiled. After which Sharon asked, "Should we not unload before we built anything?". At that point Nora looked at her three sons and Jonah who she classed as her fourth son saying "What are you standing around for? We are burning daylight" Jonah looked at Nora who was smiling winked looked at Simon, Harry and Joseph and as he started to move away shouted "**RACE YOU**".

While all this was happening Paul caught up with Leo and said " I think we need to talk" Leo at first was quiet but then nodded, Leo started " why did you leave us was it just a bit of fun you wanted" Paul replied " NO I did not know your mum was pregnant if I had known I would have been there for you" Paul continued " I know it's hard you met my wife well I have two daughter of my own" Leo was shocked on hearing this and said " so I was a mistake you want nothing to do with me that's ok" Paul stood quietly then replied " you got me wrong would you like to meet your sisters and if possible we could all get to know each other use the new East Tridam as a new beginning together" Leo hugged his dad and cried and said "YES".

Just like when they built the Ark a notice board was erected to hold the blueprints, Paul helped Alan and

Michael Tee move the statue from the back of the lorry so that it could be cemented into the hole in the middle of town that had been dug. When everything was unloaded and sorted Joseph did a head count so that the ladies knew about how many to cater for in total. That first day there were five hundred volunteers there to help.

The building work had now begun with the placing of the statue in the middle of the town a list provided by Noah of the people that died in the unfortunate natural disaster was being added by the stone masons.

Joseph with the help of Jonah devised a work plan to split the helpers that had volunteered into smaller groups so that the foundations could be dug then laid. The foundations although there were five hundred helpers, took quite a while to be laid as East Tridam might look like a small town but a lot of buildings needed to be built in such a small space. A few weeks in some of the volunteers left but to everyone's surprise as some left more would replace them. Joseph and Jonah worked well together. As the new people arrived they briefed them properly and made sure that the small groups that started each job had been refilled with new volunteers to maintain and aid the smoothness.

Noah was not getting anywhere so Nora asked if possible the first place that was finished could she and Noah have so Noah could rest. Everyone agreed. In fact Jonah split one group in half to help make a property available quicker. The first property was built and an extra-large window was put in so Noah could rest but still be a part of everything and be able to look as the town was being built.

The rest of the buildings were made to measure and built off site and brought in on lorries so all they needed was to be secured into place like a jigsaw puzzle. They arrived flat packed for easy carriage. Then when they arrived all that was needed was the framework to be connected so the brick work could be added after which the houses could have the first lot of electrics and plumbing added one house at a time, before moving on to the next after which plastering was added before a second lot of electrics and plumbing could be added.

After Six months of very hard work almost all the volunteers had left but before they went they all found time to visit Noah and shake his hand. The last place to have the finishing touches added was the all new St John's Church in which it was built on the newly named Christus Road in memory of Adam and Evelyn Christus the previous vicar.

With everything that needed to be arranged the one thing that Jonah did not find was a new vicar for St John's. Partly because he did not know where to start. Secondly, he was hoping Noah could sort that but the pressure of building the Ark and a new town was too much for Noah so Jonah did not want bother him. The new East Tridam now without the dams was completed. Simon and Sharon placed a ribbon at the replaced entrance to town while Harry and mostly Hannah brought Noah so he could cut the ribbon.

Everyone was shocked when they reached the ribbon to cut it as on the other side of the ribbon was everyone who had helped rebuild the town. The people were shouting for Noah to hurry up and cut the ribbon as unbeknown to everyone the volunteers that worked on building the town were now there to move in as they all wanted a fresh start for them and their families and could not think of a better place than there.

One of the people waiting was Nicholas De-Most who had a strange glow around him that to most would be unusual but to Jonah it was now normal. When Noah cut the ribbon Nicholas walked up to Jonah shook his hand and asked "Where is the bank?" Jonah looked Nicholas in the eyes and smiled to which Nicholas said, "Its ok, I have got enough money to start the bank with me as the bank manager if that is ok.?" Jonah looked at Noah who was sitting on a chair smiled then Jonah said

"WELCOME EVERYONE AND GOD BLESS YOU ALL".

East Tridam was again a busy town once again and with the gift of the two lorries "No work 2 hard" was back in business. Everyone was happy but they still did not have a church leader Noah's family all agreed Noah could not take it on.

After a month everybody had a leaflet posted through their door saying, **"Church opens again this Sunday"** everyone first looked at Noah but Nora stated, "It's not Noah he's been ill in bed all week, I wonder who is responsible and who is the speaker?"

Sunday morning came and Simon, Harry and Joseph along with their wives all met at their mum and dads to eat a full hearty breakfast, all except Noah who was not feeling that good but insisted he was going to church with them.

When, what seemed like the whole of the town, was seated and some standing at the back of church, Jonah walked up to the front, welcomed everyone and started to tell the whole of the town his life story from how he started off poor because of the way his parents treated him. The kindness shown by Noah and Nora when they took him in and treated him like their own in which the town folk clapped. After the clapping had stopped Jonah carried on, "My downfall came next as I preferred the love of money more than the love of a family so I turned to crime, ran a casino in town. When the going got tough I hid. While the flood was going on I realized God loved me still and Noah did love me too. Then while hiding Paul's daughters who at that time was called Saul needed my help. Paul will explain later why. When the flood was disappearing, I found God again and here I am today".

Paul got up thanked Jonah for his help then he began saying that he thought he was tough and could handle anything until he tried cocaine and got hooked so he could pay for more. He turned a blind eye to Jonah and what he was doing but I also hid away along with my family.

While the flood was going on my daughters with Jonah's help brought both me and my wife through cold turkey. When I woke up on hearing Jonah singing and praying we all joined in. When Noah's family saved us all I realized it was God's love that kept us all safe."

After he had finished Jonah got up to tell everyone what song they were going to sing and all he could see were people crying but they were tears of joy not of sadness. After a few minutes with Paula, Paul's wife on the piano everyone stood up to sing. **All things bright and beautiful** after which Mary along with Martha read from the New International Bible a passage from?

Luke 15:11-32

11 *Jesus continued: "There was a man who had two sons. 12 The younger one said to his father, 'Father, give me my share of the estate.' So he divided his property between them.*

13 "Not long after that, the younger son got together all he had, set off for a distant country and there squandered his wealth in wild living.14 After he had spent everything, there was a severe famine in that whole country, and he began to be in need. 15 So he went and hired himself out to a citizen of that country, who sent him to his fields to feed pigs. 16 He longed to fill his stomach with the pods that the pigs were eating, but no one gave him anything.

17 "When he came to his senses, he said, 'How many of my father's hired servants have food to spare, and here I am starving to death! 18 I will set out and go back to my father and say to him: Father, I have sinned against heaven and against you. 19 I am no longer worthy to be called your son; make me like one of your hired servants.' 20 So he got up and went to his father.

"But while he was still a long way off, his father saw him and was filled with compassion for him; he ran to his son, threw his arms around him and kissed him.

21 "The son said to him, 'Father, I have sinned against heaven and against you. I am no longer worthy to be called your son.'

22 "But the father said to his servants, 'Quick! Bring the best robe and put it on him. Put a ring on his finger and sandals on his feet. 23 Bring the fattened calf and kill it. Let's have a feast and celebrate. 24 For this son of mine was

dead and is alive again; he was lost and is found.' So they began to celebrate.
25 "Meanwhile, the older son was in the field. When he came near the house, he heard music and dancing. 26 So he called one of the servants and asked him what was going on. 27 'Your brother has come,' he replied, 'and your father has killed the fattened calf because he has him back safe and sound.'
28 "The older brother became angry and refused to go in. So his father went out and pleaded with him. 29 But he answered his father, 'Look! All these years I've been slaving for you and never disobeyed your orders. Yet you never gave me even a young goat so I could celebrate with my friends. 30 But when this son of yours who has squandered your property with prostitutes comes home, you kill the fattened calf for him!'
31 "'My son,' the father said, 'you are always with me, and everything I have is yours. 32 But we had to celebrate and be glad, because this brother of yours was dead and is alive again; he was lost and is found.'"

To everyone's amazement Jonah walked to the front looked down then up towards where Noah was seating just as

Noah got out his notebook and smiled. Jonah started to preach.

I am not use to speaking and I thought this passage was so relevant to how my life story earlier in this service was portrayed to you all. In the reading that was read brilliantly it's a story of a man who wants his money now and not wait just as I was welcomed into a position in a family firm I wanted the cash without working for it.

Once the opportunity came I jumped at the easy buck in the passage the father gave the son his share of the family fortune that was going to be his anyway later, I took the same route for the easy money. The only difference between me and the son was he wasted the money, the money for me kept coming in has I sold drugs to get people wasted and has the more the money came in the more I wanted as I was slowly loving money more and more, the son in the passage kept losing his money as I was making more. The only thing we both has money weather losing or making money we were both were not happy. Money was the only thing we loved and that was the only thing we both loved even more than the love of a good family. I now know the love of God and the love of a great family that we both mistreated badly but in my own life the love of God and Noah alone with his family which they all forgave me.

In the passage the son needed hit rock bottom before he realized his home and the family servants were getting better treated than him.

The way we both ended up because of God's love and the love our family. I eventually knew that I needed turn my life around and reaffirm my faith in God and give my life back to him and in turn I helped Paul and his Family to know the true meaning of love and riches and because the love that God can show people who only let him in because the sins we commit God sent his only son to die for us. With this love, we all were saved in my casino panic room as well as standing here alive to talk about it. In the passage the son even in his rag bone state as soon as his father saw him he praised God ran right up to him and welcome his son back home where they celebrated his return. On his return, thou his brother hatred him for the money for his money would now be split in two as he wasted the money so he would suffer, Noah's sons however because they had God inside them welcomed me back in to the family as if I never left. Noah and Nora welcomed me back to just has the prodical son father welcomed him back.

To finish I would like ask everyone a question, "how does the passage in the bible and what I told you about my life affect how your life his now?"
When Jonah had finished, Nora clapped then turned to Noah seeing his eyes closed thought he was asleep left him there has the final song was sung, after which Paul got up to give the final blessing.

Simon nudged his father and on not doing much in a way of waking him Joan checked his pulse and on feeling nothing realized he had passed away looking up she could not speak. Nora looked at everyone and knew he had died, Jonah on seeing them all gather around Noah, walked over to join them seeing Noah's notebook on the floor picked it up and looked at the top page and smiled. Looking at Nora he showed what he wrote then she too smiled. Everyone looked confused until Nora said "Noah has left us a final message" it says **"I can come to you now Lord I am happy and content my work here is done"**